Compendium of Coffee Table Short Ironic Metaphorical Stories

By Eric J Smith

What you are about to read is a series of short, metaphorical, ironic stories. They are meant for people that do not have a great deal of time to sit and read a novel, but do enjoy tales that they will deem, hopefully, clever and interesting in nature. In no way were these tales written to insult or demean anyone or anything, and one other caveat would be that if there are any similarities between person, place or thing that it was purely coincidental and not meant to represent anyone of these in particular. So please read with an open mind and a sense of humor.

Special thanks to my wife Amy; who is the only reason I need for everything. She also helped to edit my story's and gives me her total and sometimes unsolicited opinions.

To my two boys, Little D and N who give me hope on a daily basis for the future of human kind.

To my parents who made me who I am today. Hopefully that is a good thing. John, Michelle and the boys; love you all.

To my friends who I also count as my family; Chuck, Ed, Yogi, Jason, Marci…you all rock!

To all the crazy things that spawned my nigh insane ideas; which also helped to inspire this book and all my scrawling.

And to you, the reader, I hope you enjoy these stories and realize that, "To be bereft of humor, is to be devoid of life."
—me

COMPENDIUM OF COFFEE TABLE SHORT IRONIC METEPHORICAL STORIES
By JT Smith

Inevitable Zombie

There I was lying in bed dreaming of sweet things and nothing of importance. Not a care creasing my brow or befuddling my REM cycle. Then something stirred, something shifted that wasn't in the range of the pulses and breaths that was natural to my house. I slowly came from my slumber acknowledging something that was out of the norm. Something that seemed foreboding to my current state of being, my respite. I had a feeling I knew what it was, but didn't want it to be so. I was hoping, no…lying to myself that if I just tried to return to my slumber then it would all go away.

Scrape…clunk…clunk….

The sound was louder this time. There was no denying that I was hearing the sound indicative of a zombie. Yes, I know what you are thinking, no such thing as zombies, but you are wrong. They exist and walk among us, mostly during the twilight hours.

Scratch…clank…screech…

The zombie closed in on the bedroom door. I felt a chill permeate my entire being, not with cold but with knowledge. The knowledge that my future would forever be changed and my fealty would be altered. I also had a terrible feeling that the zombie which closed on my refuge, my bed that is shared with the woman I most love in my life was my wife. Unfortunately she was also the zombie that was closing in on our room. She exited sometime during the night and had been gone for several hours. She left to answer the call that every mother is drawn to. The call that a mother can never ignore, the one that comes from her child.

Scratch….scrap….rapp…shuffle…shuffle…shuffle…

The creature moved closer and my fight or flight mechanism kicked in, but to no avail. I realized in my heart of hearts that there was no chance to escape my fate.

I realized that time was short and the present was going to

be pivotal in what comes for the future.

I can imagine my wife stumbling down the hall way. A

fumbling mindless creature looking for a means of

fulfilling it's destiny by propagating more zombies.

Scrabble….scrabble…scrape…

I cringe in my covers trying to use them as a shield against

what will come….I know it's to no avail but I wish,

hope…deny myself the truth. The truth that my rest and

peace is going to be shattered and that my spouse is no

longer what she used to be….hell I'm no longer what I used

to be, but it will happen soon.

The door knob rattles as she numbly tries to open it; her

cold unfeeling hand trying to manipulate the door knob as

to gain entry to my refuge. And she succeeds, I am

surprised that she maintains such dexterity. The door

slowly opens and a silhouette of a small female figure

standing in the doorway wearing a night gown with little pigs on it. Little pink pigs that my wife adores…she thinks they are so cute. She calls our infant son her little pink piggy. She moves forward stumbling and mumbling unintelligible words due to her brain's inability to form cohesive thoughts.

"Mrrmrr…bo…slleeeep….cr…y…in…you…rr…ttt t.t….rr.nnn.." Her words are the death knell to my tranquility.

And so here I am…slowly stumbling down the hall toward my son's bedroom. I am now a zombie…a new parent zombie who is so tired I can't even think straight. I use the wall to steady myself and I slowly approach my sons room where he cries to be changed. And so the zombie cycle propagates itself as it does every night…for every new parent.

Buffet

It was a beautiful day, one of those days that makes you glad to be alive and able to witness the beauty of mother nature. Two friends ran in to each other at a local establishment for repast.

"Hey, hey Steve is that you?" A voice cried out.

Steve turned around, "Phil what's up dude?"

"Hey I didn't know you visited this buffet. How's it going?" Phil inquired.

"Good, good, just trying to eat quick and get back to the family." How bout you?

"About the same, trying to get a quick bite and bring some take out back to the family." Phil replied.

"How are Lucy and the kids?" Steve asked.

"Oh you know Lucy, one minute she's thrilled with how things are going and the next she wants to move." Phil attested in a down trodden tone.

"Hey I know what you mean, me and Kathy are pretty much done. I try to stay around and help out but she won't even let me near the kids. Thinks I'll hurt them or something. She is sooooo critical." Steve confided.

"Oh man, I'm sorry to hear it. You mess up once and can't ever live it down." Phil consoled.

"Tell me about it, but on the bright side I met this other woman who has this incredible body. She is something else...long legs, gorgeous face and forget about her body. Built like a champion amphisbaenian. Hell she could be a model." Steve reminisced.

"Really, wow...I really love Lucy, but at times I could totally understand looking else where. Right after the kids were born she became totally belligerent towards me. She wouldn't let me near her or the kids. Even now she told me to come here and get them some food but how much do you wanna bet when I get back she will tell me to leave it at the door and begone. Heck I even see this young stud moving around the neighborhood, he likes to stop in front of our abode while he's out, "exercising" and flaunt his youthful body right in front of us. I ought a tear his lower jaw off." Phil said.

"Damn Phil you really do love her...hell if it was me I would say keep your stud I'm off to my amphisbaenian hottie." Steve said with a smirk on his face.

"Ha, yeah I guess, um..hey Steve what the hell is an amphisbaenian? Is that like a girl on girl thing?" Phil inquired.

Steve looked confused at his friend then laughed, "Ha..hahah...you know I didn't even think of it like that. I guess it does sound similar but no that isn't it at all." Steve explained.

"Oh wait here comes the next course." Steve yelled out, "Hurry up Phil or you won't get the freshest food!" They moved up to the buffet and made sure they got their fill.

"Phil this is probably the best buffet I've ever been to." Steve said with his mouth full.

"Yeah I know what you mean....Hey you see that?" Phil said with surprise.

"What? What is it...is it Kathy? Damn she's like a stalker." Steve claimed.

" No, there is a guy over than with a camera pointed right at us." Phil said with surprise.

"What? No way! What the hell would he be taking pictures of us for?" Steve was still chewing his food.

"I don't know, maybe Kathy got him to spy on you? Or maybe Lucy has him watching me, you know she doesn't trust me. She thinks I'm messing with some youngling down the way." Phil proclaimed.

"Hmmm...well we can go over there and kick the shit out of him. Find out what he's up to and who put him onto us." Steve said with his chest bowed out and his teeth showing. Trying to act tough.

"No, no maybe that isn't it. He's near one of those jeep things anyway. We couldn't get close before he would be gone. Besides that might not be it at all. Look at the side of the jeep." Phil said.

"What the yellow box thing with the white letters in it?" Steve inquired.

"Yeah, I've seen that symbol before I think he's one of those weird voyeurs that like to watch us eat." Phil suggested.

"Yeah they are really freaky. I caught one checking Kathy out last week. Trying to get a shot of her in the raw. Fricken paparazzi." Steve claimed.

"Okay I think I will head home, had my fill and I'm ready to pop. Not to mention got to get back to Lucy." Phil proclaimed.

"What! Are you kidding look at all this food just wading through here. You only death rolled three times and you're full?" Steve was flabbergasted.

Phil rolled his nictating eyes, "Yeah I'm trying to watch my figure. Gotta compete with these young studs." Phil said and then swam away.

"You're just whipped!" Steve chastised his departing friend.

SURVIVAL

Picture a world that is harsh beyond belief in which you

could die at any second and you don't know when or

where. A world that has more dangers than it does safety

and the future is not only unknown but almost assured to

not exist for you. Death is a constant and the only reason

you may live is due to odds. This is my world and it is hell.

When I was born my odds of expiring from a lack of food

or from being murdered were better than not. My siblings

died, my parents died, my cousins, aunts, uncles, friends.

All dead, and I could ponder about the reasons, how they

died, who killed them. I know what you're thinking, that

this story is about revenge. Me going after those who

killed my family and friends. I wish it was so, but I don't

have the luxury nor the ability to exact that kind of death. I

would expire before I could find all those responsible. So,

no, this is strictly about my survival and that of my child.

My wife and other kids were murdered just like my other family was. We do what we must and survival is the only requirement because the alternative is not viable. Not if I want a future for my girl. Yes my little girl who is just now realizing that this world is cruel and harsh. She is still mourning the loss of her mother and siblings. I do as well but don't have the luxury, to dwell on my grief, not if I want us both to survive. I loved my children and my wife but I also realize the futility in languishing in their deaths. My cousin did that very same thing and then he did the unthinkable, he went after those who killed them. He was in a blind rage and charged right at them. He didn't last a second they, the killers, hit him with their vehicle at high speed. His neck snapped when he hit the windshield. All of his limbs were broken and his face was crushed inward. They didn't even slow down, it was a hit and run. Their vehicle was already in the distance and barely visible before my cousin's body stopped moving and twitching on the ground. I don't know how long my child and I will last with such horrible people in the world. Those who take life without remorse or care; those who see us as beneath them so that our own lives carry no weight on their conscience. We move as fast as we can but my little girl has trouble keeping up. She tries her best so I can't be angry, she is so small. I can't stand the thought of my little angel being destroyed by these monsters, so I can't quit and I can't surrender to the utter impossible odds. I had an uncle that submitted to the hell and torment. He quit running and stopped hiding. It wasn't so much as revenge but being tired. He attacked one of them, tried to bite him but it was to no avail. The man he attempted to assail beat him to death, beat him until he wasn't even recognizable. I don't begrudge him, my uncle, his decision because I too might have quit after I lost my dear Annette. That was my wife and she was my world. My beautiful angel who made living worth while, made the hardships easier to bare. Now she is gone, but I have my daughter who is the spitting image of her mother. She is now my only reason to continue this sojourn we call life. We sleep when we can and unfortunately we dine in the refuse left over by our protagonists. They waste so much that we can live off of their affluent and carefree lifestyles. As long as we stay below the radar and don't make our selves known to them we can exist. Being allusive is the key and I plan for us to be like ghosts. We do not stay in one location too long nor do we take more than we need to survive. Unfortunately this thinking is also the reason my child and I are close to starvation. We have been moving for several days now and haven't been able to find sustenance to keep up our strength for much longer. We hop rides where we won't be spotted and sleep in locations that offer the most cover. I notice my child starting to lose stride, she can't keep up this pace without some food. I was on the verge of giving up when I noticed our salvation. It was a dog and there was no one around it. I know what you are thinking and it may be seen as a disgusting thing to do but this is desperation and my child is more important than pride. I tell my child to hold back and follow at a distance. I don't know if this dog is feral or will attack us. I wanted to follow for a little while and see if it will stop in order for me to partake of this fortunate life saving find. The dog moves between some trees sniffing and moving about. I stalk it waiting for the right opportunity. I am too weak to chase it so I must bide my time and not scare it away. I wait for the perfect opportunity and there it was. The dog had stopped to defecate and that is when I moved in to strike. Just before moving in on the prey I motioned for my child to move up in order to stake our claim and quickly get our fill so we will not become the hunted. The dog had finished and was starting to move away when I took my chance. I moved in at high speed and was the first to strike and my child was quickly behind me. There was no time to cook our food we just engaged and then ate as much as we could. My daughter buzzed next to me slightly while I started to eat the dog shit. We would live to fly another day.

HELL

I wait, wait with the expectation of pain and suffering, I

have nothing else left to me nothing to be excited about,

nothing to be happy about and nothing to feel but empty

expectation. Expectation of what, you wonder? More pain,

suffering and the knowledge that it will never end. I wait

for my protagonist to return. Yes return, they leave and

then they come back, but no, it's not a reprieve and not a

mercy. It is just a wallowing of the coming pain. The

knowledge that it will return to inflict more suffering and

agony. This abattoir of horrors has no end and no care for

the inflicted suffering. I look to the right and left and see

the other poor souls who are in the same situation. Some

refuse to look up fearing to catch my eyes and see the pain

and loss that they feel reflected back from my visage. Fear

to look at me and each other to see the utter loss and nigh

apathy because we have, or at least those of us who have

been here long enough to realize, there is no hope. Some of the other old heads, those that have been here a while such as I, will catch a look from one another and see the horror reflected back. I caught the eye of one such poor bastard and he too had the same feeling of utter futile loss. His glassy eyes reflecting the dead visage of our painful predicament.

The real bitch of it is the fact that I can't think of one damn thing that I did in my life to deserve such a horrible hell. Such a miserable loathsome painful suffering. I'm not saying I am an angel and that I haven't done sinful things in my life, but I tried to do right. I never hurt anyone else intentionally, I never stole or did the wrong thing. I tried to live by the golden rule and tried to help others when they were in need, but low and behold here I am in a miasma of suffering and never ending torture. Sharing it with these other poor bastards, old pro's at this sort of thing, such as myself, and some young and still learning of the horrors that are to come. A few might even think they have some kind of hope for reprieve…saving….hope where there really isn't any. Poor dumb bastards, they fool themselves and really don't know but they will, yes they will know.

Experience has taught us what not to do such as to never, ever, allow those who inflict the pain know that you are feeling the pain. That is when they explode, that is when the pain intensifies a thousand fold. It is imperative to feign interest in what those who inflict the pain are doing. To show that we are okay with the suffering and actually tell them how good they are at what they do. Yes I know it's masochistic to encourage the antagonists who are responsible for our suffering but if you don't then your pain will be that much more. And so I hear a newbie, a rookie, make that fateful choice. I hear him do the unthinkable and I cringe. A pang of sorrow and sympathy go out of me for the dumb shit. He groans which is the worst thing he could have done because just as he issued his complaint, just as the auditory mutiny voided his mouth, the sadistic antagonist issued forth and then the fireworks began. All of us cringed at the hail of pain and suffering that fell upon the dumb ass. The poor shit never realized what he was doing until he did it and now he will never forget it. The rest of us cringed as the assault reached a nigh deafening crescendo. The guy right next to me faced his pain bringer as the antagonist entered right in front of him. Still I felt for the man, but he took it in stride and even showed thanks and gratitude to his abuser. Never once did he show his pain, never once did he relent under the tumultuous onslaught. A feeling of pride went through me. I felt it for him, because if he can resist the desire to relent under the flagellation and pain then so can I, just as these thoughts entered my mind it was my turn. My sin eater entered in front of me to delve out my next round of turmoil. And as it opens it's gullet straining to engulf my soul I hear the mocking mantra that is the same every damn time…that same cliché.

"So, what do you think? The red one or the white one? I think the white dress makes me look fat. What do you think?" my wife asks, of me.

"No dear, they do not make you look fat. I really like them both." And so the man next to me beamed his approval toward my ability to keep myself from cracking under my wife's endless questioning of how her clothing fits. As if my true answer could be allowed, that would be my death knell. To say, "No dear the white one doesn't make you look fat. They both make you look fat!" But I would never say this for my death would be painful and slow. So we, the husbands, sit in a row outside the dressing rooms and wait for the pain to begin again.

PENDING DEPTH

Somewhere in the Pacific, deep within the depths of the
worlds largest ocean sits a vessel who's very design was to
bring silent and unbeknownst death. A machine that was
engineered for one purpose and at this very moment the
tables were turned. This machine and her crew hover far
above the ocean floor but also just as far below the surface.
At this moment the Captain awaits his final moments
before a pending and ever immanent explosion eviscerates
the hull of his ship and cavitates all the oxygen and himself
into the embrace of oblivion. The idea of being blown out
of his own submarine by exploding forces and then just as
quickly compressed by the depth was unsettling to say the
least.

He ruminates about the loss of the entire fleet; which
occurred just moments before the dire situation he has
found himself to be in. First they lost the air craft carrier, a

massive ship that could easily be mistaken for a city on water. The numerous sailors it housed, and the machines that would expel forth, it birthed them before they would undertake whatever missions they were sent upon and would take them back into it's embrace where they could find sanctuary and refuge before being set forth once again. Many called the air craft carrier home, but not this Captain. His home was not on the waves, but below them and now the very place he called home was also to be where he would be interred, his sarcophagus. The next ships they lost were the patrol boats. Their enemy was smart in taking out the carrier first, the weapon was fast and swift, no time to react and no time to salvage. The carrier went out so fast that there wasn't time to save anyone, and then the patrol boats were next. The same devastating weapon, as best as the Captain could manage to describe it, was like a giant red projectile from the sky that pierces the very heart of the ship and then plunges it into the blue depths. So fast and effective that the entire battle group had no recourse and no escape. The destroyer started firing it's main battery of guns, but it was a vain attempt to lash out at anything. More of a last death rattle before impending doom descended from the heavens and struck it down. The red spear plunged deep and more followed to be sure of the destruction wrought on the destroyer was total. Oh how the tables turned and now the Battleship was facing the inevitable. She tried to turn, maybe she was running from her fate. Maybe in a futile attempt to spot an unseen enemy, but all for naught. The Captain of the submarine watched through his periscope as the red giant dropped from above. He wondered what kind of plane could hold such a massive weapon; a weapon so immense that it's very weight mixed with the force of impact was enough to drive it's victim to the bottom of the ocean. The insane aspect of it all was that the weapon didn't even explode it just impaled and then drove down it's helpless victims.

The Captain realized with fear and awe that they were the last of the battle group. Only this lonely small sub was what remained of a once mighty group of destruction. This amalgamation of powerful destruction that was being sent forth to inflict fear and subservience from whomever they were to be unleashed on. And now some unknown enemy with a power that could not be from anything conventional was the predator and they the prey. He was unfamiliar with this role; even when he was in a different battle field long ago. Another war which he was thrust into in another place and time when he was a younger man. That war wasn't fought on the ocean but on the continents. It was a world war and it was bloody, he lost many friends and nigh lost himself in that war. But they did prevail and he would never forget the sacrifices and risk involved. It was risk and he was the taker but somehow managed to pull victory from the jaws of defeat. He would never forget the giant

Roman numerals that would also descend from above. Maybe whatever force had driven those numerals to crash on the very earth they were fighting upon was the force responsible for this impending doom. He thought to ask why they would see fit to spare him then only to deliver his demise now at the bottom of the ocean. Then a noise rented the quiet fearful silence his submarine was bathed in just moments before. The captain felt the ship lurch forward and he grasped for something to hold on to while his ship was being impaled. Before his very eyes he witnessed the red spear plunge into his submarine's control room and just before the ice cold grasp of death took him he could hear a loud voice yell B-9 and sunk! You wanna play Risk again?

MEMOIRS OF A MASS MURDERER

What makes a man do the things that he does? At what point do we deem what is wrong and what is right, and who deems it so? What kind of epiphany can make a man leave his home one day and walk into a crowded restaurant and kill everyone in sight? Or climb into a bell tower and start shooting indiscriminately. Could it be something so profound that only a select few could understand what he or she is thinking at the time? What possess a mother, the most sacred of guardians, to kill her five children, or put her two little boys into a car and drive it into a river? Is it a spoon dropping on the floor, or a raindrop hitting a windshield? Maybe a song that plays on a radio or a movie that shows a certain scene that flips the switch turning a would be normal individual into a killer. Is it genetic, or some kind of damage one sustains during their life that creates the abominations, as society sees them, who can kill those that don't deserve to be killed? This is a story about brothers, about family, and about killers. This story will show how such abominations can come about, and given the proper imputation can thrive and be utilized as a weapon.

I am just one of those people, but unlike the individuals who get caught I kill thousands and never see the inside of a cell. Bundy, Dahmer, Gein, Fish, the Rostov Ripper, Jack, they are all amateurs who let their emotions get the better of them. They made the mistake of making it personal. Killing those who match a certain category, or a trait that flicks that switch. I'm a killer, a murderer, and a taker of life. I kill without mercy or conscience. Genocide is my creed, and pain is my mantra. When near I become the death knell ring for suffering and carnage in which none escape my path. I poison, crush, and lay traps for my pray. I am the reaper of those who sow their own fates. I work for any who pay my fee and I exterminate with extreme prejudice. Women and children stand vigil, frozen at the morbid sight of my deeds, waiting for the cacophony and massacre to end.

Different names, or titles have known me, through my many years of service to death. I have been a vivod to those I have expunged from this plane, a Potentate, a vengeful God. Their lives I have taken and rarely spared. Spared, not always by whim but for job security, for if I destroy all of my victims then there shall be no one in the future for me to kill.

Now I find myself at another doorstep. I prepare myself for the dark and bloody work ahead of me. It isn't personal, just business. I am a whore of death, an incubus for the unwitting masses that await my judgment and sentencing. And there in the dark enclave of my next employers and victims, I hear the heralding of my encroachment. The sweat and innocent voice of a child, a small angel. "Dad the pest control man is here."

And so the cycle begins anew, and I hear the crescendo

building. Killing is my business and business is good.

RUMBLE

I can remember when I was younger, much younger than I am now. I was a strong man, a strapping man, a man others would either envy or shudder in my wake. I wasn't too smart when I was younger, I was in a gang and not just any gang, but the baddest group of cut throats you would find in these parts. There was a large number of us, well large for that time period and particular place. We were the bad boys of the town, nobody would mess with our tight knit gang. Until our rivals showed up; they thought they could horn in on our turf, but they thought wrong. I was known as Mr. Big, because I was tall and muscular…well I already explained my physical presence. Then there was Wheels; he was fast and the best damn wheel man around. Next we had Blade; excellent with knives and he had something of a lisp. There was Stinky; he was in our chemical and biological warfare department, he could stink up an entire building if he was ripe enough. Then there was The Stilt he was our man for some hand to hand combat. Finally there was our leader and our gangs name sake; T-Bird. T-Bird was a deadly man who could out think the best of them, his mind was very sharp. Maybe it was the antidepressants he was on, but it didn't matter how he came up with our strategies and planning just that he did it with zeal and prestige…a leader among men. We used to be known as the Seven Deadly Sins; even though we were only six. Our seventh man was Petey, ah but he had a bad heart. One gang bang too many and he had a massive heart attack. So here we were at our local hang out when our protagonists walk in. Our new nemesis was this gang calling themselves The Scirtaireg. Weird name if you ask me, I think it was code or something, but that was neither here nor their. We looked them up and down checking out their roster of players. They had a leader like us, hell there is always a leader, a center. Then they had their own wheel man, and it looked like he had a custom rig just like our guy. There was one, a Mexican, I think he was twirling a butter knife that was on the table a minute ago, just like our Blade. He probably had a lisp of his own. This was looking bad, they even had a guy just like Stilt, and you could tell he was an itchy one just waiting for action. They had a larger fellow just like me, except he had something of a belly on him. He even had a fancy contraption on him that he carried in a bag. It was a metal cylinder with a tube leading to his nose. I thought " I better watch him he might use that as a weapon on me. Just what I needed an oxygen junkie."

Then there was their leader he was a scary looking guy. Half of his face looked slouchy and he walked with a limp. He had an evil eye that probed us, and the other eye kind of stared off into the distance.

T-Bird was the first to speak up, "Why don't you assholes go back to where you came from. There's a bagel shop down the street you scallywags…or whatever you call yourselves, you can go haunt that joint."

We cheered T-Bird on, and snickered to ourselves saying, "He called them scallywags." That gave us a good laugh, but they weren't laughing, in fact the tension grew in the restaurant and everyone began getting ready to square off.

Their leader retorted with his own comment, but his speech was slurred and muffled.

The little Mexican guy stepped up and translated for their leader.

"Our esteemed leader says use guys can kiss our white….uh….our different colored assess."

Yep he had a lisp all right.

T-Bird responded "Why don't you make us ya gay blade."

Then he looked over at our Blade and apologized. Then the shit really hit the fan. Their Stilt man, the one with the itchy trigger finger was the first to make a move. He lunged, well maybe not lunged but moved, in our general direction. Stilt, our boy, cut him off and they clashed. Wheels was next to throw down and he matched off against their wheel man. They resembled a movie I once saw called Ben-Hur, with sparks flying and their custom rides smashing into one another. Then the big guy made his move at me, and just like I thought he used the tank on me. In fact I think that was what they called him, Tank. I ducked his swinging tank as if it was a mace in some medieval movie...or like Kurt Douglas in "Vikings"...great movie that was....I remember I was with Betty Boskipsky at that showing....boy did we have a good time....oh wait the rumble. So Blade, ours, had already thrown one of the butter knives near him and almost struck the Mexican, except he was off about five feet and really

struck a bus boy. Probably due to Blade having cataracts
and a limp wrist, but he was still very fast….just not
accurate. I wonder why Blade never married…he was a
handsome man…always dressed in nice clothing… was
clean…hell back then most woman would find that an
endearing trait…oh wait the fight… The fighting was
intense, but the end came as it must when their leader fell
in defeat to T-Bird. It was our proudest moment, our
triumph over our rivals for our much coveted turf. The
fight was epic and T-Bird's defeat of their leader would be
one for all ages. My eyes were sharp and their man Tank
was out of the fight since he threw out his hip trying to
swing his tank at me again. I was able to watch T-Bird take
down their leader. The carnage in the restaurant had us
banned for life, but it was worth it. T-Bird was incredible
he walked right up to their leader, I think they called him
The Stroke or maybe it was Winky, my memory isn't what
it used to be, anyway T-Bird walked up to the Stroke and

dodged a really slow punch, that would have missed him anyway, and T-Bird just pushed The Stroke down. The Stroke never got up, he just lay on the ground and shook a great deal…probably from fear. They ended up calling an ambulance for the Stroke….seems he was having one. Wheels had destroyed the other guys wheel chair, and our Blade was out cold, due to the Mexican having better aim with a salt shaker. Stilt and their stilt were stuck. Both of their walkers were interlocked and jammed. They were just cussing at each other on the other side of their walkers. Oh and Stinky, who was odd man out, well he was outside because he stank so bad we didn't let him in the building to begin with. If he wasn't going to wear his depends then we weren't hangin with him. We successfully defended our turf, our Joe's Surf and Turf to be precise. We were still the baldest assed 76 year olds around. That is until we got our asses handed to us at the bowling alley by a bunch of Quadriplegics. The little bastards were half our ages and we didn't have Stilt with us. He suffered another fall and we didn't need two wheel men. So here I am now the last of the T-Birds at age 87 remembering the good old days of my youth. Oh wait a minute Wheel of Fortune is coming on in the day room I gotta go and beat up old man Stevens so he doesn't change the channel.

Disorder

Cletus was not what you would call a savant. In fact he would almost prove the theory that there is a direct correlation between visual Cro-Magnon esque features and mild mental retardation. Cletus knew he was lacking in proficiency when it came to education; school was never his strong point. He was always a big kid who slouched naturally and gave the illusion that his knuckles would drag the ground if he did not lift his arms. Cletus realized his future did not include physics, biology or math. Cletus went for what he could understand in life and that was military. His father was a disciplinarian who would whip him if Cletus ever stepped out of line. A drill sergeant was just another father figure for Cletus. Unfortunately for Cletus it was the height of the Vietnam conflict. Cletus was in the thick of it, and he learned the mantra of his platoon without faltering, "Kill or be killed." Cletus did not revel in the death, but was efficient. He took his lessons and extrapolated what needed to be done in whatever situation was provided for him. Cletus was a survivor, but not the type who kept his head down and survived by luck, no, Cletus was the type to kill the enemy before they could kill him, or his platoon. Cletus would volunteer to go ahead as a scout and with stealth born of a one track mind and simian esque strength Cletus would eliminate the enemy snipers, or diffuse ambushes before they could strike his platoon. His Lieutenant would use Cletus as the point of a sword to penetrate the enemy, and with the rest of his Platoon as the belly of the weapon to cleave through what Cletus had started. Cletus was called the "Helper", Cletus's Lieutenant gave him the nick name, because, he claimed he was sent by god to help him and the rest of the platoon make it through the hellish jungle combat. Cletus loved his nickname and his Lieutenant. They gave him the acceptance he was looking for, the place he needed to be and the meaning for his life. He could remember many a time when his Lieutenant would yell

"Helper get up here and clear out that nest of

Charlie, they dug in deep and we can't get them out."

"Charlie", that was the enemy that pervaded Cletus's

mind. Charlie was his enemy and Charlie would die at his

hands. Cletus was the only one in his platoon that loved

what he was doing and where he was, until one fateful day

out on one of their sweep missions. The Lieutenant was

out front and Cletus was near the rear of the platoon. The

lieutenant told him to take it easy and relax, they didn't

expect any real resistance. Cletus did not like this idea he

pleaded with the Lieutenant to allow him to do

reconnaissance out front of the platoon. Cletus seemed to

have a sixth sense for finding Charlie, but today the

Lieutenant wanted his pseudo adopted son to take it easy

because he feared Helper would get burnt out. They were

walking through some thick monkey grass when the first

bullet whistled past several of the men in the platoon.

Helper was stricken with fear that he had failed his friends and his father figure. Cletus quickly worked his way up the platoon line, ignoring the metal projectiles flying past him at incredible speeds. When he reached the front of the platoon line he found his pseudo father, staring blankly at Helper. His eyes wide with shock and a gaping hole residing in the center of his face. The Lieutenant was dead, and Helper had failed his father. Anger welled inside Cletus and he charged the Charlies who had killed the man he considered the closest thing to a real father he ever had. Cletus was hit several times, but he accomplished what he had set out to do. There were fifteen Charlies in the group that killed the Lieutenant and all fifteen died at the hands of Helper. The wrathful helper sent by god to smite Charlie for killing his pseudo father.

Ten years had passed and Cletus was checked into an institute for the mentally insane. After the wounds he had taken and the loss of Lieutenant Cletus was never quite the same. He tried to function in normal society and until he lost his temper at a fast food restaurant he was working at, he was surviving just fine. The arrogant man on the other side of the counter was screaming at his wife. He was calling her all kinds of names and profanities were spewing from this sinner's mouth. Cletus turned from the grill where he was cooking burgers, because Cletus was never quite smart enough to run the cash register. It always came up severely short when Cletus attempted to run it, and he would get flustered trying to match up the food item with the correct button on the machine. Cletus was frowning at the man who was screaming at his supposed wife and the man noticed him. All the other fast food workers and costumers were looking away from the scene, afraid to get involved. Cletus was not afraid and the man took notice.

" What the fuck are you looking at ya retard?" The man espoused from his filth ridden mouth. "Just cook the god damn food and mind your own business." Cletus just stared with anger brewing in his eyes.

"Charlie leave him alone he isn't hurting you." The wife spoke up.

The man raised his hand as if to slap the woman across the face for speaking to him in such a manner.

Cletus looked at the man and the woman and the name echoed in his mind over and over again. "Charlie" he was the enemy he was the one who killed the Lieutenant.

The woman cringed and closed her eyes expecting the back hand she was about to receive from her abusive husband, but the blow never fell. She slowly opened her eyes when she heard a different kind of noise and that was when the screaming started.

Her husband was on the ground on his back and his eyes were wide open with shock, just like Lieutenant's eyes when he died. The difference was that the man's head was perforated between his eyes with a knife that was used to cut onions and various restaurant items. In fact the knife in

Charlie's head smelled distinctly of onions. Cletus had once again killed Charlie. Cletus was sent to a mental institution and resided there for ten years after that incident.

"Doctor Bailey I am telling you we have to make room for more patients and as far as I can ascertain Cletus has come along nicely. He has shown the ability to interact with his peers and has not succumbed to another bout of rage since the incident that placed him into our institution."

"Director do you even know what that incident was that placed Cletus in our care?" Doctor Bailey asked.

"I have many people coming and going from this institution and it is impossible for me to retain that kind of knowledge on someone who has resided here for ten years."

"He killed a man who was ordering food from the fast food restaurant where he worked."

"Well has he shown any signs of that same behavior since?"

"No, but that could be attributed to his medication."

"So we give him a healthy supply of his psychotropic medication and a prescription, as well as after care with social workers to make sure he stays okay and we send him on his way."

"Sir I would like to go on record as saying that this is a bad idea. Cletus is only stable due to his medication. When he came into our institution he was ranting about killing Charlie. The name of the man at the restaurant was Charlie and Cletus is a veteran of Vietnam. He is unstable and could cause a great deal of harm given a certain stimulus."

"My decision has been made Doctor. You will release Cletus today and give him a healthy supply of is medication. Do we understand each other?"

"Yes sir." With that Doctor Bailey spun on his heal and left the Director's office.

Cletus was released from the hospital with, what they call a healthy dose of his psychotropic medication; which he could not even pronounce. He was slightly dazed and had difficulty concentrating. Cletus walked with his duffle bag over his shoulder with no destination in mind. His parents had died while he was institutionalized and he had no siblings. His aunts and uncles were very distant from his family when he was growing up and he didn't even know their names. Cletus had no where to go and no one to turn to so he walked.

The Quickie Mart on the corner of 5th and Main was not the best place to be at midnight on a Friday night. This particular convenience store has been robbed fifteen times in the past year. Debra needed gas and the place was self serve so she scooped up her little girl who was barely awake and entered the store. The store was quiet and the clerk was behind the register, but something was different. The clerks eyes were wide and they looked as if he had

seen a ghost. Debra did not like the way the clerk was
looking at her and decided to back track the way she came
into the store. She was halted when she ran into something
that was behind her. When she turned she was shocked at a
tall man wearing a ski mask and wielding a shotgun. Debra
clung tightly to her daughter who was dozing. The child
was straddling her mother with her head over her mother's
shoulder. The man motioned for her to move toward the
rear of the store where the clerk was sweating profusely.
As Debra neared the counter she noticed another masked
gunman who rose from a crouch behind the counter as well
as three other people who fell victim to this robbery. There
were two women and one young man and all were
crouching on the floor with the gunman behind the counter.
His pistol was trained on the Clerk.

     "Alright the two of you move around the counter
and get on the floor. Time we finish our business and go."
The clerk sat on the floor as well and Debra slowly lowered

herself to the floor never letting go of her daughter.

"Alright Billy let's get the money and go." Said the small man with the pistol to his accomplice.

"Shit man why you use my name dammit!!! Now we gotta waste these bitches to keep from being found out." Yelled the big man with the shotgun.

"Dumb ass we gonna waste these bitches anyway to keep from anyone describing us." Protested the smaller man with the pistol.

"Then why the fuck are we wearing these damn ski masks?" Said the big man.

The people started crying on the floor and Debra clung to her daughter and sobbed. She would not wake her daughter because it was probably more humane not to let the child know about what was about to happen.

"Because ya dumb shit we want to be careful in case the cops show up."

"Alright well let's get this shit over with I don't like

killing anyway." Said the big man with the shotgun.

The two men moved around to the opposite side of the counter so they would not get the full blood spray on themselves. Just before the firing commenced the door chime rang out announcing a new arrival to the store. Both men spun around and pointed their weapons at the doorway, but there was no one there.

"What the fuck was that?" said the big man.

"Go check it out." The smaller man instructed. The big man moved toward the door and then around one of the isles. That was where he found Cletus holding his duffle bag and staring at a box of tampons as if the answer to life's most difficult questions resided within the box. The big man looked at Cletus and noticed how disheveled Cletus appeared to be.

"Hey man what the fuck are you doing?" Said the big man.

Cletus slowly turned his head to acknowledge the large

man with the shotgun who leered at him. Cletus meant to say something but when his mouth opened to utter words collected saliva came flowing down Cletus's chin. The doctors had given him too much medication and Cletus was a walking zombie. The whole world was moving in slow motion for Cletus and he could barely make a cohesive thought.

"So what the hell is it?" Yelled the smaller man with the pistol.

"Hold on I'm bringing our new arrival back there. You gotta take a look at this guy." Returned the large man who was laughing at Cletus.

He nudged Cletus to the rear of the store and near the counter. Debra could make out the disheveled homeless man who was obviously retarded. She felt pity for the man as well as her daughter. Neither would understand, nor even realize why their lives were about to end.

"This guy is some kind of retard or something. He

was staring at a box of tampons over there like it owed him something." The big man laughed.

"Are you a fucking retard dipshit?" Said the smaller man to Cletus.

"Hey man put the shotgun barrel in his mouth I want to see if his brains look different than these other shit heads." The smaller man commanded.
The big man was reluctant but did as he was told. The barrel of the shotgun entered Cletus's mouth and he slowly sucked on the end of the tube.

"What the fuck is he doing." Said the big man.

"Ya got me this guy is really gone. Go ahead and empty his head out."

"No please don't." Cried Debra. The other people were sobbing loudly now; knowing that their time was nigh.

"Come on Charlie why I gotta kill a retard it aint like he can tell on us." Pleaded the big man.

"Just fucking do it."

Cletus heard the name Charlie and something in the recesses of his brain began to spark. Some deep recognition, and his eyes dilated a little more. Cletus looked down and noticed the woman clutching the child in her arms and the woman was saying something.

"Please god help us." Debra cried waiting for a miracle.

Help….help…Helper…that was Cletus, he realized. Cletus was Helper and this man in front of him was Charlie. Cletus moved with lighting speed. No longer were the drugs retarding his physical abilities and his training returned. Charlie must die and Cletus was god's Helper sent to do just that.

The large man was surprised when Cletus grabbed the end of the shotgun and spun the weapon around using his own arm as a pivot. The barrel was now pointed at the big man's face and Cletus, The Helper, helped the man's fingers to depress the trigger. The big man no longer had a face to speak of. The smaller man was shocked and started to run for the door, but he was Charlie and Charlie could not live. Cletus pointed the shotgun at the fleeing man's head and discharged the lethal weapon. Charlie was only a few inches from the barrel of the shot gun when it discharged and now Charlie's face, brain, and skull was streaming down the wall of the convenience store.

Cletus was returned to the institution for mentally insane people, but was treated differently. People that worked in the institution treated him with respect and Cletus was visited often by a woman named Debra who brought him home made pies and assorted goodies.

THE FEUDAL SAMURAI

The time frame is feudal Japan. The setting is a massive battle to decide the future ruling class of the entire island nation. The field of battle is littered with the bodies of fallen Samurai, men who bravely fought to the death for their lords. In this battle there was a distinction between what people of the time would call good and evil. The good are a culmination of several clans who pooled their might to face the onslaught of evil. The evil clan led by Lord Nobunaga; Oda Nobunaga a notorious feudal lord who would rule the land with an iron fist. The scene was playing out as a tragedy. For every one of Nobunaga's Samurai who fell in battle, three of the opposing Samurai would perish. Nobunaga was a tactical genius who was using all of his wile to crush this once massive army beneath his forces. This last battle would solidify his reign over Nippon. He first used his mounted samurai to confront his enemy and once taken some losses pulled back the mounted forces through a nearby valley. The enemy, thinking they had the Oda on the run, gave chase. Once the mounted samurai were through the valley, Nobunaga's archers unleashed a nigh never ending hail of arrows upon those who had entered the valley. When the raining death had ended the Oda's infantry rushed over the hills of the valley to massacre the remnants of the enemy. After this slaughter was finished the enemy believed Nobunaga had committed all of his forces to the trap. The enemy, with what was left of their forces charged into the valley to attempt to wipe out the Oda inside the valley. Nobunaga was no fool, he sent the majority of his mounted samurai in a huge arc prior to the trap in the valley, around to the rear of the enemy. The result was a slaughter of the opposing hierarchy from the various clans. Once the Oda mounted samurai dispatched the leaders of the opposing clan they were to ride down on the army that was attempting to destroy those of the Oda who were inside the valley. This would be a pincer movement to catch the enemy between the two forces and finish them once and for all. The only fault with Nobunaga's plan was the unexpected arrival of Heromasa. The Ronin Hero of Nippon who was regarded as Nobunaga's equal in battle. Heromasa realized what was occurring in the valley and reigned his forces back in order to avoid the deadly hail of arrows. Heromasa guided his soldiers around the hills of the valley and toward the opening on the opposite end. Waiting at the mouth of the valley was none other than Oda Nobunaga the demon Lord. Heromasa rode on toward the demon and his remaining forces. Nobunaga caught sight of his nemesis charging down on him and his remaining samurai. Nobunaga turned his attention and his forces toward the new threat. The battle was intense and the Samurai were battling in heavy armor in the mud; which was making the ongoing struggle grueling. They were fighting with their swords in a macabre dance of death. Heromasa was carrying his way through the Oda as if they were so much fodder. His sword was crimson from the life fluid that sprayed from his enemy. The ground was becoming saturated with blood and viscera, not to mention the corpses and limbs. Heromasa was a master of martial arts as well as the sword and both were coming into play in his dance of death. Heromasa cleaved through the Oda samurai as if they were children attempting to attack a Tsunami with straws. Lord Oda sent his elite guard to kill Heromasa. He did not wish to risk the highly skilled and personally picked warriors to fight Heromasa, but they were all that were left to him. All of the Oda that were with Nobunaga were now dead. The closest Oda samurai were entrenched in the battle with the other clans. The positive side, for Lord Nobunaga, was that only Heromasa remained. Heromasa's men fell to the Oda as well.

Heromasa faced off against the ten Samurai who comprised Nobunaga's elite guard. With their swords in front of them, poised to strike the blood soaked Samurai in front of them. Heromasa glared at the men with eyes of pure fire with an intensity that these men had only seen in the eyes of their Master and Lord, Nobunaga. They knew that they were now at the card table and death was the stake; Heromasa was the dealer and the deck was loaded in his favor. The first of the Oda elite moved with a downward slash to cleave Heromasa from his head down. The only problem, for the elite guardsman, was his bowels. They had exited his body and were now strewn on the ground in front of him. In the second it took for the man to strike the ground dead three of his comrades were following his lead to the ferryman. Heromasa was faster than any man had a right to be. Nobunaga looked on as the last of his elite were dispatched by a God. Now he two faced the Ronin's blade.

Heromasa would finally avenge the death of his master. Before him was the Demon Lord himself and the blood soaked warrior God, Heromasa who was fearless. Though Nobunaga was renowned as the Demon Lord of the Oda, Heromasa did not waver, for what is a Demon compared to a God? Their swords locked and sparks rained. They parried for several minutes and it was obvious to Nobunaga that he was a great military strategist, but lacked the ability to utilize a sword like his opponent. With several deft moves Heromasa had disarmed Nobunaga, of his sword, and was preparing his signature death strike to finish the Demon Lord when Heromasa stopped. Heromasa's eyes grew wide and fear ran through his mind.

"No not again!" Cried the Samurai. Heromasa had frozen in place while Nobunaga smiled at his fortune this day. The mighty God of war Heromasa failed to kill the Demon Lord. No, it was not due to any weapon, or fear of

Nobunaga, nor anything Nobunaga had done, but it was due to a 10 year old boy. A 10 year old who was too tired to hit the triangle button. Daniel had fallen asleep while playing his favorite game "Samurai Gods". Heromasa would have to fight this battle all over again due to the 10 year olds inability to stay awake long enough to see its end. And so the battle for feudal Japan continues another night!

THE CONMEN

"Listen Mrs. Wilbur if you do not send us a check for the three hundred twenty two dollars and sixty cents that you owe us we shall have our attorney prosecute you!" Joe listened to the excited and hysterical voice on the other side of the line with a smile on his face.

"Sir I don't understand, our medical plan should have covered those expenses." Pleaded the old woman.

"Ma'am we have tried to reach you several times and we just don't care about your reasons anymore and we shall sue you for the amount of money you owe us, unless you get a check on my desk in six days!" He raised his voice so as to convey his seriousness.

"Okay, okay there is no reason to take us to court we can pay the bill. Where do I send the payment?"

Joe smiled and gave a thumbs up sign to Roger, or was his name Pete today? He sometimes had trouble remembering which fake names they used on what days.

"You can send the payment to Collections Inc. PO Box …….."

"Well another successful con. And that Roger…or Pete…or whatever your name is this week, is how it is done." Joe smiled his patented shit eating grin.

"It's Brad."

"Brad? Who's Brad?" Exclaimed Joe confused.

"My name this week is Brad, dumb ass. Hey don't you ever worry about getting caught, either by the police or the people we con?"

"Hell no, I already told you ya shit head, we have an answering service receive our calls, and they don't even know where we are located, and we use a P.O. box to avoid people knowing our true address. Plus we have the computer to tell us the number of the people who call us so we can screen it. It is perfect, and besides you know we only go after old people or widows. They are so easy to scare." Joe said triumphantly.

"Yeah I just worry, I know what you're saying though. Yeah, I'm cool with it. Hey did you see the one I got this morning. Mrs. Giovitti, she sounded hot."

"Oh really, well you know our business has a no fraternizing with the people we screw policy. Hahahaha" Both men laughed.

"Shit you should have heard her Joe. I think she was ready to pee her pants. I claimed she owed us ten grand, but we would be willing to accept three payments of a thousand."

"What, are you nuts?" Cried Joe, "You think she can pay that amount?"

"Ha it was funny, but then she started to sound as if she didn't believe me. So I really put on the whole sue her for everything she owns bit. You know she even claimed she would speak with her husband regarding the matter. Like that would scare me, hell we know she's a widow it says so in her medical file we pulled off the internet. Stupid cow thought she could scare me, ha."

"So what happened?" Joe was intrigued and also wanted to know about the money that this poor widow would be sending in.

"I called her bluff and told her to have her husband call me back." Brad said and folded his arms.

"Okay well has she called back yet?"

"No she claimed her husband would call me back at two this afternoon."

Both men looked up at the clock in their apartment/office. The clock was nearly two now.

"Well I hope you can pull this one off, because that would be just enough for me to take my vacation to Hawaii this year." Joe said with greedy eyes.

"Yeah and I wanted to check out those new flats over on the east side. I think that would make for better arrangements for our business here." Brad kept his eye on the business.

"Maybe we could go legit and open a real collection agency after we get a nice place like that and some money under our belts." Brad was hoping Joe would go with his plan for legitimate work rather than this illegal shit they kept dabbling in.

"What the hell are you talking about?" Joe boomed, "Why the hell should we give this up? We make a shit load of money, tax free, and with none of the risks that a business would offer. What the hell do you have against our set up now?"

"Look nothing lasts forever. We will eventually be caught. The smart money is to take what we have and turn it into something legit." Brad pleaded with Joe hoping that reason would win the day, but to no avail.

"Bullshit you chicken. This is the best fucking thing we could do and you're trying to ruin it. I'm telling you no one can find us. Now I'm going to go get today's checks at the post office. You man the phones."

"Okay, okay and pick us up some take out will ya, I'm starved."

Joe left the office and slammed the door on the way out. Brad knew he was arguing with a wall when it came to Joe and his business ventures. If something worked, then why fix it. That was Joe's motto.

The phone rang, waking Brad out of his thoughts.

"Hello."

" Is this Brad?" A mean sounding Italian accented man asked.

"This is Brad." Brad retorted with the same bass added to his voice.

"Yeah, well this is Mr. Giovitti I'm calling because yuse is giving my wife a hard time today on the phone. Claiming some bullshit about owing yuse some ten thousand clams. What the fuck is this shit about?"

"Yeah well Mr. Giovitti, or whoever yuse is," Brad

said mimicking the Italian accent, "yuse ain't fooling no one. We know that Mrs. Giovitti is a widow and that she owes us payment of ten thousand for medical bills that were turned over to this collection agency by the doctors who gave her service. So I was going to cut her some slack and allow her to pay installments, but after this I do believe we shall sue for the full amount." Brad said with a smile on his face. That was good, he thought, he sounded like Joe with his threats. He felt confidence in himself, confidence that he could pull this huge con off.

"Listen here ya little fucker, yuse is mocking the wrong guy. Now I am Mr. Giovitti and yuse is pulling the wrong shit with me. So tell me smart guy what are the fucking bills from, since my wife nor myself see an outside doctor."

Outside doctor? This baffled Brad a little. What did this guy mean by an outside doctor?

"She knows what bills I'm talking about Mr.

Whatever your name is. If you keep this charade going I will have you in court before the month is through."

"Okay ya little fucker I think I'm onto this shit. Yuse is trying to con me out of my money. You are some kind of con man trying to extort money from me. Ha that is really funny ya little fucker. You don't know who I am do you?"

"I don't really care who you are. If Mrs. Giovitti doesn't pay us the money before this week is through Iwill take legal recourse against her." Brad was raising his voice to the point of yelling. This guy was taking it too far. Usually people got scared and did what was asked of them..

"Okay, you wanna play this game fucker, I got yuse. Yuse and your little buddy." Then the phone hung up.

'Little buddy?' Brad thought, 'How did this guy know there was more than one of them?' Brad traversed the floor from his desk to the window. Five stories below he could see a few people, in the depressed neighbor hood they lived in, mulling around the street. Nothing out of the ordinary. But what the guy said really bothered Brad.

"You and your little buddy?" Brad said to himself. "And what is that shit about knowing who he is?"

Brad calmed himself down. Joe would be back soon and he would tell him about it. Maybe they could think this one through, or maybe this was the time to bug out. Cut their losses and move on. Maybe this guy was some kind of cop trying to flush them out. 'Shit what if the cops are onto us? Fuck I sure wish Joe would get back here.'

There was a knock at the door and Brad jumped. He controlled his fear and moved slowly to the door. Brad slowly put his eye to the peep hole. And was shocked when the door was struck with a loud rap.

"Come on Brad ya slow ass open the door for Christ's sake." It was Joe.

Brad let out a sigh of relief.

He undid the chains and the locks and as he was opening the door it was pushed violently open.

Joe was standing their glaring at his slow partner.

" What the hell man, what took you so long to answer the fucking door?"

Brad noticed that Joe wasn't alone. "Who's that with ya."

"It's Dave man, I saw him down town near the post office and decided to get a dime bag from him for tonight. He asked if he could come party with us and I said what the hell. Why you got a problem with Dave?"

"No I don't have a problem with Dave, but we have an issue to discuss regarding our business and I don't think this is a good time to get wasted." Brad was tensing his jaw and giving Joe his irritated look.

"Dude whatever the deal is it's okay, Dave ain't fucked up with it." Then he pushed past Brad and entered the apartment with Dave in tow.

Brad stared incredulously at Joe and then slammed the door.

"Crash anywhere Dave." Joe said ignoring the slamming of the door.

Dave picked the multi-patched somewhat smelly and definitely from another era, couch and sank into it. He pulled out the weed and some rolling paper.

"That's Dave, he always gets down to work, no small talk." Said Joe, amused.

"Hey Joe we really need to talk, I had an issue with a patron today." Brad was still pressing the matter.

Joe gave into his friends pestering. "Okay, okay let's go into the kitchen. .

What the fuck happened that has you so damn scared?" Joe inquired.

"I received that call from Mr. Giovitti regarding his wife's bill." Brad said trying to be secretive.

"I thought you said she was a widow. And so the

fuck what, even if there is a Mr. Giovitti what the hell can he do to us?"

"Man it seemed a little fucked up. The way he was talking to me….it seemed like…well like he was either a cop or something else. And then before he hung up he made a comment about getting me and my little buddy." Brad was starting to get frantic again.

"Dude the guy is fishing stop worrying about it, he's got nothing. Hell even if he is a cop so fucking what he can't find us, ya pussy." Joe admonished his friends panic.

"This was different Joe, we have been threatened before, but this guy was different." Brad said almost whining.

"Okay look you tell me how the hell they can find us, we are unlisted, our phone is through an answering agency, they don't even know our address and I'm careful as fuck about not being followed when I return from the post office. So stop your worrying." Joe was getting agitated again.

" Okay, okay I guess we can worry about this later...maybe after Dave leaves." Brad said with a sarcastic tone to his voice.

"Yeah whatever ya chicken shit." Joe said as he left the kitchen.

"Oh yeah Brad, I forgot to tell you that Pete's coming with some pizza too, so don't shit your pants if there is a knock at the door." Joe yelled back into the kitchen.

Brad could hear both Dave and Joe laughing at his expense.

"Fuck you Joe." Yelled Brad who was highly agitated.

RRRRRRIIIIINNNNGNGGGG,

RRRRRRRIIIIINNNNGNGNGGGGGG

The phone broke into their argument. Brad reached the receiver and lifted it to his ear.

"Hello?" Brad said into the receiver, but there was no answer. "Hello, who's there?" Brad asked again, but still no answer. "Hey what the fuck do you want?" The reply to his request was a click as whoever it was hung the phone up.

"What the fuck." Brad exclaimed frustrated.

"Dude it's the cops coming to get you through the phone." Joe said with an eerily voice, mocking Brad's concern.

"Man, you can go fuck yourself for all I care." Brad said.

"OOOOhhhhh no Brad doesn't love me anymore!" Laughed Joe.

Dave was a little too wasted to even laugh, he just kind of stared into space with a grin on his face.

"Dammit Dave couldn't you have waited for me? Now I got to roll my own. Dammit dude you better leave enough for everyone ya pot head."

Brad just shook his head in disgust at the apathy Joe was showing for this problem.

They sat around for a while smoking dope and watching television, when there was a knock at the door. Brad jumped up and stared at the door as if it was possessed. In his mind he was waiting to hear the mantra, or battle call of "Police" and then the door splinter in on itself as armor clad mp5 toting swat rushed into the apartment. But there was no yell, no door splintering in on itself, nor swat team members with itchy trigger fingers. Instead there was another report at the door from whoever was patiently waiting on the other side.

"Damn Brad are you going to get that or piss in your pants?" Joe harassed his friend again.

Brad didn't even bother retorting. He just moved slowly toward the door and stopped when another knock echoed from the door. Brad could hear Joe and Dave chuckling behind him.

"Jesus Christ man I'm fucking hungry if your not going to get the damn door I am." Dave said as he took incredible effort to raise himself from the couch. Dave pushed past Brad and went to the door, but even in his stoned haze he was paranoid enough from Brad to look through the peep hole. As he did so Joe uttered a squeal of laughter from the couch.

"Ha haaaahahahahahah Brad's paranoia is catchy. Even stoner Dave is scared."

Dave ignored Joe's heckling and continued to peer through the peephole.

"Hey it's alright Brad it's just Pete." Dave yelled as he could see his friend Pete looking at him, but Dave noticed that something wasn't quite right. Pete's face looked different and his eyes looked concerned, or even fearful. This perplexed Dave, but was really confusing to the stoned individual was when Pete moved back from the door way and the view through the peephole was replaced by a cylinder, a black cylinder that slid over the peephole to completely cover it. By the time Dave registered what the cylindrical object was, his eye and a large portion of his brain matter blew through the back of his skull. There really wasn't much noise, to Joe and Brad it sounded like someone had stomped on the floor really loud, or dropped a large book. Dave's body hitting the floor made more noise and the door crashed inward. Pete came flying through the door as a very large man tossed him like a rag doll through the entryway. There were three men that entered after Pete. All three could have been the missing link. All three wore black suits with black leather driving gloves and all three looked like they were meaning business.

Brad was frozen in place where he stood. Some of Dave's brain matter adorned Brad's pants. He was in shock at what had occurred. In fact none of what was happening registered in Brad's nor Joe's head. They froze as a deer caught in the headlights of an oncoming truck. Pete was alive but crying on the floor. He didn't even bother rolling

over or getting up, just cried into the carpet.

"Gentlemen." Spoke one of the three simians

pretending to be men in suits.

"Now that we have your attention I would like to inform

you that your little company here has made a grievous

error. Mr. Giovitti was called from this local and informed

that he owned someone here money. We are here to rectify

that mistake."   "Look man whatever

he owed whoever consider it paid off. Just please don't kill

us." Joe cried from the couch.

Brad just stood there shocked at what had just occurred.

Dave's brains were all over his pants.

Pete kept whining and crying on the floor face down. It

sounded really pathetic especially since Pete's nose was

broken and blood was pooling around his mouth.

"Oh for pities sake shut the fuck up." Said one of

the killers. Then he moved his hand with the silenced

semi-automatic pistol and expended another bullet. Pete's head bounced on the carpet and smegma from the new hole in his head splashed into the air and then rained back down onto the carpet and Pete's now lifeless body.

"That's better, I hate fucking whiners. Ok where was I? Oh yes, Mr. Giovitti does not like being threatened and especially having his wife threatened. So now you two must accompany us to have a little visit with Mr. Giovitti." Brad was still standing still as a stone when one of the large gorilla men grabbed him up like he was a rag doll and walked him out of the apartment. Joe was escorted, so to speak, by the other anthropoid. The third, who was the spokesman for the trio, was the last to exit, but on the way out he left a little present near the door. It was enough plastic explosives to blow the entire floor from the building.

Joe and Brad were tossed into the trunk of a very large car. A Caddy Joe believed, but the type of car wasn't the largest concern for the two gentlemen. The largest problem they were facing was the inevitable leaving of the trunk and into whatever nightmare awaited them. Joe couldn't help but notice there was something next to them in the trunk. Something that looked like a bunch of full trash bags, and something that stank really bad.

Brad turned in the trunk to face his friend; even though there wasn't enough light to see him.

"I fucking told you there was something wrong you stupid fuck."

"Oh okay now is the time for I told you so right? Fuck that Brad you were the dumb ass who called the lady in the first place. Out of millions of people you could have picked to fuck with you pick a fucking mob boss's wife." Joe retorted.

This shut Brad up, and Brad turned back around in the truck to look at the hood. He was trying to find a way out of the trunk; and then he remembered his key chain. He reached into his pocket and pulled out his key chain that he had put one of those small mini lights on. He pushed the button and it illuminated the trunk.

"Hey alright Brad, at least you can do one thing right."

Brad didn't respond but turned the light on the trunk looking for some way to get out. Fear raced through him at the sight of scratches all over the inside of the trunk hood. It appeared that others had tried to escape this same predicament.

"Shit." Echoed Joe looking over Brad to see all the scratch marks on the trunk.

Brad noticed something on the floor of the trunk near the opening. When he placed the beam on the object he felt nauseous. It was a fingernail, a bloody fingernail that was left from the last unfortunate person to inhabit this trunk. Brad for some odd reason thought back to his time spent in college. He always loved mythology, why didn't he pursue something in mythology or became a teacher or anything but another hit for a mob boss. The trunk of this car, he thought, which basically came down to be the ferry taking lost souls to the other side. The three Neanderthals were most like Cerubus guarding the way into hell and they were to be Ceribus's snack.

"Hey Brad turn the light over here there is something next to me and I got to know what it is." Joe said to his ex-friend.

Brad rolled over and put the light on top of Joe's shoulder shining it on whatever Joe was regarding now. The object was covered with green trash bags and all wrapped up. Joe manipulated his fingers into a hole he created in front of him and as he tore the bag open an un-godly smell accosted both of the men. Joe reeled against Brad when he realized what was in the bag, but Brad was still in the dark.

"What is it Joe?" Brad inquired trying to peer over his ex-friend to see.

"You don't want to know dude." Joe choked back as he felt the vomit rise in his throat.

Brad was able to manipulate the light enough to see into the hole and there staring back at him was a human, or once a human. A man who had succumbed to the simian killers in the front of the car. There was coagulated blood tracing a line down from the man's forehead over the bridge of his nose and his right cheek. The man expired from a new hole that occupied the center of his head. A crimson shakra for a man who was well into the next world.

Both men began to sob and look frantically for a means of escape, but to no avail for the simians had done this many a time and knew their business well.

The car halted and the two potential victims heard the doors open and then close. Foot steps echoed through the trunk as the three bi-pedded simians came for their victims. The trunk opened, Brad and Joe were lifted with way to much ease out of the trunk and escorted into a building that was obviously under construction.

There were two other simians waiting inside the building and between them a man sat in a folding chair with a cane in front of him. The man was looking at the two sobbing men with disgust.

"So these are da fucking maronie's that thought they could fuck with me. Me Mario Giovitti." Giovitti stood up and moved to the two cowering men. The gorillas pushed both men down to their knees.

"You two fucking punk ass bitches tried to pull one over on me? I who have eliminated Dons, and I who have risen to the point where I run this city. There isn't a fucking illegal act in dis state that I don't have my fingers into and you two fuck turds try to screw with me and my wife." Giovitti moved in a circle around the two men who were reduced to blubbering and begging for mercy.

"Stop your fucking crying and whining. You did your actions and now ya pay da price. I must say you two

have some big balls to attempt something like that on me."
Giovitti said changing his demeanor instantly.

"I can almost admire the sheer audacity to do something like that, but then I remember that it would take a fucking leech to feed off those who are helpless. The elderly, the wives who don't have much after their bank accounts have been drained from the hospital. It would take a fucking mooch to do such a thing."

Brad opened his mouth to contest the accusations, "But sir you are a criminal also you do those kinds of things yourself."

Giovitti raised his eyebrows up in response at such a statement and then looked at one of the gorillas. The look was all the simian needed to strike out at Brad for such a statement. Brad dropped to his knees when his teeth switched from one side of his mouth to the other.

"Now from my understanding the brain trust behind this little endeavor, the leech, is Joe. So which one of you little pud fuckers is Joe?"

Brad looked up from the ground into Joe's eyes and immediately felt dread. He knew that Joe was a coward and underhanded. He knew that when it came down to life and death Joe would sell out his own mother. He only had to look into Joes eye's and know the truth of the matter.

Joe looked back up at Giovitti and said without falter, " He's Joe I'm Brad sir."

Giovitti looked at Joe and then Brad then he looked at one of his gorillas.

The bullet penetrated the upper bridge of the nose piercing the nasal cavity and then passing through the skull into the soft flesh of the brain. The bullet obliterated the medulla oblongata and made an exit through the rear of the victim's head. Joe hit the ground with a sickening thud and the blood and brain matter soup made a sort of halo behind his head. Brad was stunned at the sight of Joe's cadaver. He thought for sure he was the one to die, but this was a surprise and something else dawned on Brad. From here on out he was now Joe, Brad was dead according to Mr. Giovitti and for the rest of Brad's life, however short that was, he was now Joe.

"So now there was one. Brad was the bitch who spoke like a fool ta me on da phone, but you Joe, you had the brains to come up with this fucked up con yuse two have been running. So I think to myself I have a few loose ends that I could use someone to help me with. Someone who probably could appreciate my situation. So here is da thing Joe yuse is gonna sign some papers for me, or you end up like your friend Brad here. I am not a fucking animal here so I will give ya a few minutes to think it over."

Giovitti became quiet as did his minions, but they stared at Brad, who was now Joe, for what seemed hours, but in essence was a few seconds.

"Okay time is up Joe yuse either agree to my terms

or spend eternity with your friend here in a cement block, never let it be said that I aint fair."

"What would you like me to sign sir." Brad said behind crushed teeth and blood that was seeping from his mouth.

"Well I'm glad you are sensible about this Joe, and it just so happens that I have the papers right here." Giovitti reached into a brief case and extracted some folders filled with paper. Giovitti looked up at one of his henchmen and the man proceeded to drop to all fours acting like a pseudo desk for Mr. Giovitti.

"Come here my boy, I am about to enrich yuse. Yuse is about to be da proud owner of a Laundromat and a gas station."

Brad looked perplexed but adhered to the order to come closer to the man on all fours. Giovitti handed Brad a pen and one of the Neanderthals put the muzzle of the silenced weapon to Brad's temple.

"My men are very protective." Giovitti explained in case Brad had any bright ideas about using the pen.

"Oh and by da way Joe, sign da name Brad when yuse put ya John Hancock on da documents. I don't like liars eitha, do yuse really think I didn't know he was Joe. I might be an old Guinne, but yuse don't become the head of a la cosa nostra family by being stupid."
Giovitti said with a smile. A smile that embodied pure evil, Brad had entered hell and was now making a deal with the devil. He didn't really think he would be owning, nor running a gas station, or a Laundromat. He was right, both businesses were absconded by the police in a raid. The Rico act allowed them to take both businesses and Brad was sentenced to eighty five years in a federal penitentiary for money laundering, racketeering, illegal gambling, and the possible murder of an ex-friend who they never did discover the body of.

THE INEPT EYE

Morning was breaking over the pristine and quiet campus where our story commences. Edmond, a cop wannabe security guard, had received news that there was a police test taking place in a small city within the State of Kentucky. This municipality whence the test was to take place was at least a five hour drive from the campus. Edmond had worked third shift the night before and was already exhausted, but knew that this was a one chance deal. So Edmond requested that his friend JT who also had worked the night before accompany him on this sojourn of sorts. JT, having no real life other than school and work, decided to skip his classes and join his friend. After loading up on carbohydrates at a local surf -n- turf restaurant they began their trip toward the small city. The trip to the police test was uneventful, other than to stop every twenty minutes for caffeine and the subsequent urine breaks. Edmond and JT both took the police written test and even though Edmond had done better on his written test than his friend, JT was approached by a police officer who had given a portion of the test and asked if he needed help passing the next phase. JT later reasoned with his friend that the reason the police officer took notice of him was most likely due to two facts. One being that JT was built like a small truck, and two that Edmond could not see out of one of his eyes. This kind of angered Edmond, but he remained quiet. The two started backtracking through the rural highways that had brought them to their destination. The sun was retreating behind the Earth and night was falling on their little black car. The conversations were more or less inane in nature. The current discussion had something to do with Nazis and their regime. Edmond claiming that you had to respect such a power for uniting the war torn Germany, and the kind of control they mustered. JT arguing that they were fascist scum who should have been eradicated for what they had done. Then JT noticed his friend pass a semi truck, the odd thing that caught JT's attention was how his friend had passed the truck. Edmond applied his breaks after getting in front of the truck so the truck had to break to avoid striking the rear of the little black car.

"What the hell are you doing? Did the trucker piss you off or something?" inquired JT.

"What are you talking about?" replied Edmond.

"I mean you just put your breaks on and almost made us into pate."

"Dude I'm just driving normal." Edmond said with agitation in his voice.

"Are you shitting me? Ok I noticed some discrepancies with your driving and now it's time to voice them. First I notice you break when you pass someone once your in front of them. Then I notice you stop at stop signs and wait for a car that may be two or three miles away to pass by. You also stop at green lights and then proceed. You speed at the wrong times and slow down where you can speed. What the hell is up with your driving?"

"That's just how I was taught, alright?" Edmond admonished his friend.

"Who the hell taught you…." JT noticed the semi that they had passed moments ago now sidle beside them. The odd aspect of this was the fact that the truck was slowly trying to occupy the same space as them.

"What the fuck is he doing?" cried Edmond.

"My guess would be that he is running us off the road for pissing him off." JT responded in a stoic voice of triumph. Even at the possible even of their death in a horrible car wreck, JT obtained some satisfaction at being proven correct.

"See you shouldn't piss off truckers. They will fuck

you." JT added.

The car was now spitting dirt and grass as they were now on the side of the road.

Edmond had retained control and was now behind the truck. Edmond then flashed his high beams at the truck.

"Oh what the hell is that going to do? Tell him that he just ran us off the road, big deal he knows already." JT said sarcastically.

"Just shut up." Retorted the defeated Edmond.

"Okay so tell me dude, who taught you how to drive like Mr. Magoo?"

"My mom, okay."

"What? Your mom?" JT said with surprise and humor.

"Yeah so what?" Edmond responded sounding hurt and defensive.

"You are talking about your mother, the agoraphobic, alcoholic right?" JT laughed.

"Hey don't talk bad about my mother." Edmond said, but in a more defeated tone since he knew it was true.

"Dude she didn't even make it to your wedding." JT was not done rubbing it in.   "Let me get this straight, not only can you not see in one eye, but you were taught how to drive by someone who's an agoraphobic and an alcoholic. Hahahahahahahaaaaa…..oh shit that's funny and sad." JT was having too much fun at his friends expense.

"Hey dumb ass which is more sad the fact that she taught me how to drive and I can only see out of one eye, or that I'm driving us?" Edmond said with a grimace on his face.

"Oh that is sad." Responded JT.
Both men fell into silence while they drove along the long and mostly deserted highway. The truck that almost killed them was the only vehicle they had seen in an hour. Then JT noticed out of the corner of his eye that there were lights

off to the right behind some trees up ahead. These lights he noticed were in a triangle formation and their were three of them. The lights rose into the air and moved over the highway in front of their car.

"You seeing what I'm seeing?" Said JT to his friend.

"Yeah, but what the hell is it?" Replied Edmond. The lights moved in perfect triangle formation without swaying from inertia, or making any type of movement, then they moved back over the trees and down where it looked to have originated from. The men could not make out what the lights were attached too.

"I don't think that was a helicopter." Said JT.

"No, I don't think it was either. It moved way to fast and too smoothly to be a helicopter." Edmond added.

"So what the hell was it?" asked JT rhetorically.

"Don't know."

"Well shit man let's stop and check it out." Said JT

excitedly.

"I don't know dude. We are both very tired, it could have been a trick of the eyes." Edmond said trying to reason the unexplained lights.

"Bullshit dude that was some kind of secret government shit, or a UFO. Come on ya chicken shit let's go check it out." Taunted JT.

"Okay, okay." Edmond gave in..
The car turned around by crossing the median through a dirt access path. The kind highway patrol use.

JT saw the drop off of the pavement and responded to his friend, but too late.   "Watch out dude the pavement drops....oooofffffffff." The bottom of the car scraped the pavement and jarred the occupants.

"Shit." Yelled Edmond.

"Another one of your mothers lessons?" Laughed JT.

"Shut up." Retorted Edmond as he dragged the car

onward and back over onto the other side of the highway. The car slowly backtracked to the spot where they had seen the lights and again crossed the median. They parked car on the side of the road with the hazards flashing. Both men moved in the direction of where they saw the mysterious lights. They moved through the trees quietly toward their goal.

"Come on Edmond let's go before they leave."

"That might not be a bad idea dude. I mean what if it is some top secret government shit going on. They might decide they don't want anyone to know about it. We could become expendable." Edmond's conspiracy theory paranoia was surfacing.

"Dude what if it's Sorority Babes from beyond. You know that B-rate stuff where they are looking for two guys to help repopulate their planet which by the way is full of model esque babes." laughed JT as they closed in on their quarry.

"   Keep dreaming dude." Chortled Edmond.
Suddenly they were bathed in light, and to both men's
surprise they were frozen in their tracks. Blackness was the
next stage of this bizarre adventure for the two travelers.
JT awoke to an ache in his neck and eyes, ears, back,
fingers, toes…hell his whole body hurt.

       "What the hell." JT said with a start as he opened
his eyes. He could not move because he was literally
pinned down. Their were pins inserted into his arms,
fingers, legs, feet, eyes, at the corners, and two large metal
dowels in his ears and he was naked. There were machines
all around him that were orchestrating this hell that he was
going through. The pain was searing into his skull, and
Sorority Babes from Beyond was the last thing on JT's
mind. In fact the pain elicited only one desire and that was
death, release from the excruciating pain he was in.
JT emitted a guttural scream of horror at his unfortunate
predicament. He resembled an insect trapped on a board,

pinned for future examination. Their were voices just out of sight. He could not understand what the voices were saying due to the fact that the originators were aliens. They were extraterrestrials, the kind that people speak of in cheap tabloids with large eyes and nigh translucent epidermis. These creatures seemed to be debating JT's current state.

"Juma I believe we made the right choice. This one seems to be a fine specimen, but the other had one optical receiver that was damaged. I believe the queen will be receptive of this morsel." Said one of the two aliens.

"Yes Jedmo we made the right choice, the other was definitely flawed and would have been rejected for the feast. I told you that shiny lights attract these creatures, they are the perfect lures." Informed the other alien.

The ship moved upward and out of the stratosphere. And back on Terrafirmer Edmond woke next to his black car, just in time to see the craft move at incredible speeds towards the black blanket of outer space. Edmond noticed that his friend was no where around him. For some reason he knew his friend was gone. So why was he still here? Why wasn't he taken as well.

"Oh that's just fucked up. It must be the eye, just like the damn police. They don't want me because of the stupid eye. Well I hope JT has fun repopulating whatever planet he's off to." And with that Edmond returned to his car to traverse the rest of the trip alone feeling left out and defeated due to his eye.

IN THE BEGINNING THERE

WAS AN END

It was a dark and stormy night. Dark would not begin to describe the utter blackness that surrounded the small town in the middle of nowhere America. Our scene starts in a graveyard, where there is a non indicative movement. The source of this strange and uncommon movement is the Earth right in front of a tomb stone. Lightning cracks the sky and at that very same moment a hand rips through the ground into the cool fresh air. Slowly the creature rises from its womb of cold, worm infested Earth into a world that will know that this was the night whence death visited unbound, waiting to sup on the teat of humanity. The creature is a zombie, but once had been a successful business man named Bill. Bill has risen on this night several years past his expiration date in order to full fill one need, one goal that will not rest inside what is barely left of his mind.

'Kill, eat, kill, eat, kill, eat…..and get some new clothes.' Bill used to be some kind of fashion designer. The creature, once free of its supposed eternal resting place, moves in a slow cathartic motion towards the lights of the town and the fresh bodies that he is drawn to.

'The heat, the warmth, the tender flesh, must eat, must render flesh.'

Bill tries to move as fast as he can, but being that his body is so far into decay and rot, he moves slowly. Some of his bones are showing through the leathery carcass that once was a healthy body. Bill doesn't dwell on the way he expired, on a piece of a fast food chicken sandwich that lodged inside his throat and suffocated him, he just desires flesh. The piece of chicken long gone inside his throat, but that does not matter being that Bill no longer requires oxygen, especially since his ribs are wide open to the air and most of his organs have long since been digested and discarded by worms.

Bill finally enters the street outside of his cemetery and continues on toward the town unbidden. The town is alive with the bustling of it's residents who are shopping, eating at restaurants, and doing all those things that Bill will no longer enjoy, but he'll soon fix that.

Bill enters the main street of the town through a darkened ally and notices several flesh bags walking on the side walk in front of him. They don't notice that their end is nigh, the very man who used to clothe them, in high fashion, was now here to claim their lives. He shall become the reaper of death, the very harbinger of freedom from their pathetic lives. For some reason Bill knows that once he bites one of these pathetic automatons he would spread that gift that has been bestowed upon him. He would be the epoch of the end, and the alpha for a new world, and he has spotted his first victim....I mean convert for his new world. A young boy stands close to the alleyway sucking on a sucker. Bill thought this to be appropriate seeing that he was soon going to be sucking on the boys brain stem in much the same manner.

Bill moves forward into the pseudo light that rains down from a street lamp above. Some of the people surrounding the street notice the arrival of the desecrated figure that now reaches out for his first kill.

Bill's hand, or claw now that most of the flesh has been ravaged away, grasps around the boys arm. The boy spins around to see who has gripped his arm with such a disgusting feeling, as of a piece of coarse leather. Much to Bills chagrin the boy screams and his eyes become very visible due to the receding of his eye lids. People surrounding the street scream in chorus as well. Music to Bill, his new theme music, or mantra for what he will reap on this world. If Bill had lips he would have a great big smile, but only a few pieces of flesh still traverse the distance between his jaw and upper maxilla.

But suddenly Bills reverie is taken away for the crowd stops screaming, as does the child who would be his first victim. Bill looks at the child and notices he is looking down at his arm and then Bills after world comes unraveled. Bills desiccated arm is still hanging onto the child. When the boy had spun around Bills arm became unattached to his shoulder. Now Bills arm and hand is hanging limply from the boy. This was not good, the boy looked up at Bill and smiles, for it dawns in the child's mind just how different the situation has become. No longer is he, the boy, the hunted or the prey; but now he is the hunter and he lashes out at Bill kicking him hard in the shin. Bill does not feel pain, but to his dismay his barely flesh covered leg, well not really flesh covered more like sporadic pieces of flesh hanging onto his bones in a pell-mell manner, flies behind him and lands several feet away. To Bills horror the crowd is laughing at the scene and more people gather around to see the show.

      'No this isn't a joke, I'm the reaper, the death bringer, evil incarnate. I'm a FU#@'N zombie for pity sake. How is this possible that a mere child is destroying that which I was to sow.'

Then the child, now goaded by the laughter of the crowd and like all children loves the attention, latches onto one of Bills ribs and begins to pull. Bill realizes his plight, as he hears his rib separate from his corpse, that this gift given to him should have gone to a freshly passed individual and not one who has died years prior. The boy has now removed most of Bills ribs from his torso and laughs at the one armed, one legged, balancing zombie who now is no more a threat to him as a new born baby would have been, but then, that is what Bill is. A baby who has just been born, and now this cruel and heartless world chastises and destroys this child of death, but much like a live baby who could still scratch it's parents eyes or skin on their fleshy faces, if the parent isn't careful, so too can Bill. The boy laughed with a wide open mouth and did not realize that a small piece of Bills desiccated flesh, and the very particles of powdered flesh that sheds from Bills rapidly discombobulating form, has entered the boys body and in three days time after the child becomes ill and then passes, he shall bestow Bills legacy upon the world, he shall be the incubus for the world to suffer.

And so ends Bills after life as the crowd assists the child and finishing the wrenching of long since dead bones and flesh. Soon after Bill finds his head, and pieces that were found near his head, reside in a glass tank inside a lab being studies by scientists. Scientists who continually poke and prod Bill, but soon Bill shall have his revenge. Soon the world will be besieged by the masses of dead who shall feast on the living. The world shall be born anew.

THE TAKING OF INOCENCE

The setting is the old west. The time is high noon, and the
place is a small town in the middle of nowhere. People are
stirring about the town with their everyday business, but
unknown as yet to them death has entered their town.
Death rides a pale horse and goes by the name of Sid. Sid,
or Death, or the Ferry man, or just plain evil. Sid has killed
more people than he can remember, be it full grown men,
woman and even children. If it had lived at one time or
another Sid has ended it.
The first townsfolk at the edge of the one street town
noticed Sid entering on his horse, moving at a slow trot.
They stopped what they were doing, everything had just
become useless and inane to them. They had come to the
realization that today just might be their last. There have
been stories of Sid making whole towns of people

disappear. Stories of him executing everyone who annoyed him. There was no mistaking who he was either, Sid wore the same type of clothing where ever he went. A black pair of pants, black shirt, black boots, black hat and a blood red bandana around his neck. He had several guns adorning his body, and if each gun could tell a story everyone of them would have a novel by now. There were wanted pictures everywhere of Sid, but no one would ever act on them. His bounty was over 100,000 American dollars. That was unheard of in that time, but no one has ever been able to collect and no one has tried in a long time.

The people were watching Sid's slow progression through the town's only road and some stopped with their jaws dropping, others dropped their belongings. Woman held their babies tighter to them and began praying. All normal activities in the town had halted, even the dust seemed to slow down to avoid Sid. The people would have run, but they were frozen by fear; and they also knew it was futile to run from Sid. If he wanted to he would go through each building to find them and exterminate every last one. The most popular question running through everyone's mind within the small town was "Why is he here?". Rarely, in fact it was never really heard of, did Sid leave a town without killing someone. So who's day was it today, who would meet their maker on this day? How many would join them today on their route to the maker? The Sheriff raised his hand up slowly, not to reach for a gun, but to cover the badge on his chest with his hand. He barely warranted a look by Sid, and the killer just continued down the road toward an unknown destination. Maybe he was just going to the saloon for a drink, or the barber for a hair cut? It didn't really matter because someone was going to die this day. People had tried to kill Sid, but obviously no one was successful. Even the military had searched for the right hand of Death called Sid, but he always disappeared before they could get him, or killed entire groups of men.

He was the deadliest man alive and this town knew it. If a person even had a gun out of it's holster Sid would not hesitate to kill that person. He believed in eliminating all possible threats. Be it a Man, woman, or child if they had a gun out in sight of Sid they died.

This was the deadly folly that a father realized too late. The father was across the street coming out of the barber shop and noticed his eight year old son on the other side of the street playing with a gun. He had told the boy time and time again to never touch his guns, but for him, like all boys the lure was too great. The revolver was his extra rig that he kept under his saddle in case of an emergency. The real emergency was now riding up the rode on his pale horse toward the man and child. The father knew he could not cross the street in time before the killer would see the boy with the gun. The father called in a choked whisper that he hoped would reach the boy in the deathly quiet of the town. "William, William put that down now boy." The boy was engrossed in the weapon and did not hear his father. William kept turning the gun around and kept trying to cock the hammer on the weapon. His little fingers struggling with the heavy hammer, under developed muscles strained to make the gun cock. The boy just wanted to see what the gun would sound like when he dry fired it, but the killer would not know this, nor care. Sid rode ever closer and the father was panic stricken now. Several other people on the opposite side of the street from the boy also noticed the child's mistake, but all were too afraid of Sid to yell to the boy. The Sheriff also noticed what the people were staring at. Suddenly courage flared within the Sheriff, he knew that the killer would not hesitate to extinguish the child's life. The sheriff started moving forward toward Sid; he was thinking that if he shot the man in the back no one would fault him. The killer was a monster, he had killed women and children. How could he hope to stand against the man in a fair fight when even the army failed to take him down? No, this was the way to do it, one shot in the back and then another into the rear of his skull. The sheriff started to move his right hand to his gun, and then it was too late. The killer noticed the child and the revolver that was being cocked. Sid moved with lightning speed and removed his death dealer with nigh inhuman speed that no man could achieve. The child also looked up at the noise of the approaching horse and realized that something was severely wrong. The father across the street cried out as he knew he would no longer see his child alive. Then there was a piercing noise that made everyone flinch. The shot was fired and the woman around the scene started crying. The bullet penetrated the eye first; then passed through the occipital nerve and severed the connection with the brain. Next the bullet passed through the gray matter in the frontal lobe, and soon traveled passed the pituitary gland, but did not rupture the gland. The projectile exited the top rear of the skull, creating a huge exit wound. Sid fell dead from his horse. The child had accidentally discharged the gun in his small, once innocent, hands. Everyone was in shock, this nigh immortal killer, this death bringer, the scourge of all lawman, felled by a single bullet from a gun that a child was playing with. The people moved their gaze to the child and noticed that he too was shocked and awed at what occurred. A tear started to move down the child's cheek. He was scared at what this implied for him, he had just killed a man with his father's gun. His father was the first to reach the boy and grabbed the child up in his arms. The father embraced his son and held him tight; soon after the crowed surrounded the father and son and began cheering. The boy was confused at this unexpected event. He had just killed a man and these people were happy and excited for him. He felt a strange rush of excitement and adrenaline at the same time. People began to talk, and soon the word was spreading of the little boy who killed the killer. "Little William had killed a man who was feared by all." They said. "William Bonnie the kid of only eight years old killed Sid the renowned and vilified monster of the west." was touted on newspapers around the entire country. Some called the child nicknames "William the kid, or even Billy." His own moniker.

VACATION

Bill prided himself on being what he considered slick. Bill

was boarding the airplane and feeling a smug satisfaction

on his cleverness. A few weeks ago his company was

offering a vacation package to the sales person with the

highest sales for the quarter. Bill knew his lazy attitude

would never permit him to strive for such a difficult goal.

Selling those little disks that companies put in their urinals

for supposed sanitary purposes was not an easy sell. Bill

had just finished training a young man who was fresh out

of school and looking to make something of himself. This

kid was breaking all records and Bill knew that he was

going to make the goal for sales, but Bill was smarter than

your average toilet cake salesman. He knew that while the

young man was in training his sales would go under those

of his trainer. The young man would not actually be given

credit for his sales until the trainer turned him over to his own route with his individual sales account number. Bill neglected to switch the young man's number over from his own and so Bill accrued the other's sales. Not only did Bill win the trip, but he was given a fat bonus for record sales. Bills picture was placed on a plaque at the main office, and he was the talk of the toilet cake industry. Bill entered the place from the causeway wearing his loud Hawaiian shirt and khaki shorts. Bill smiled at the flight attendant as he she greeted him through the door of the plane. The attendant's smile faded quickly as Bill patted her on her backside. "Sir." The woman retorted to the unwelcome touch. Bill smiled at her and continued on to the rear of the plane. Bill thought back to the young sales man he had trained. The look on the poor kids face as he witnessed the president of their company shaking Bills hand and congratulating him on a job well done. The young man had narrowed his eyes suspiciously at Bill, but had no proof of the deceit that made everything possible for Bill. Bill just smiled an innocent smile and acted shocked at the news. Bill had made sure to give the young salesman his own account number a few days prior to the end of the competition. Hell even if they caught on Bill could care less. It's not like he couldn't find an equally boring job somewhere else, or he could plead ignorance to the mix up with the account numbers and his winning of the contest. Either way he would win. Bill took his seat and waited for the plane to leave the tarmac. He lit a cigarette and relaxed into his seat, pushing the button to recline.

"Oh excuse me sir?" A voice came from behind Bill.

"Could you please move your seat up, you're hitting my knees, I haven't sat yet."

"Yeah, yeah whatever lady." Bill replied in his apathetic voice.

Bill moved the seat up for roughly a second and then hit the button again to recline.

"Oh sir, please."

Bill ignored the woman this time and shut his eyes. The woman strained against the seat and adjusted herself while scoffing at Bill.

Bill drifted off to sleep even before the plane took off. He awoke to the sun shining through his window seat and when he looked out the window and down he saw blue water. They were heading South over the Gulf toward paradise. A few hours later the plane was touching down on good old terra firma. Bill exited the plane and was staring at palm trees and women in hula skirts.

'Wow, Bill thought, just like Hawaii.' Bill had no real plans except to check into the hotel and relax on the beach. A man dressed like another tourist was standing next to a pillar, had taken notice of Bill.

"Bill? Bill from Toilet Cakes Ltd?" Bill stared at the man preparing to run in the opposite direction.

A million thoughts racing threw Bills mind. 'How

the hell did they figure out what I did already? How did they get down here to catch me? Wait a minute this guy seems surprised to see me.' Bill calmed down, but narrowed his eyes to study the other mans face. Nothing came to mind.

"Bill it's me Ted from the Burbank office. How you doing."

"Oh Ted yeah, I'm good what are you doing down here?" Bill played off like he remembered the man. The truth is Bill is so obtuse that he couldn't be bothered remembering anyone who did not immediately have a use. Bill was all about helping Bill.

"Oh I'm here on a vacation trip to see this dynamic speaker my wife has been going on about."

"You bought tickets and came all this way to see a speaker." Bill was floored by the crazy idea. To expend the kind of money it would have taken to come to this place just to hear some guy speak.

"No, no this guy's group actually paid for the trip. He even has a town named after him. He's some kind of super rich and smart guru. I'm telling you this guy is something else. Hey you know what why don't you come to the lecture today and hear the guy out. Maybe you could get invited for the next seminar."

Bill thought about the invite. What the hell? He might need another job when he gets back to the toilet cake world. Besides maybe he can find a way to extort some money out of this guru guy.

"Okay when do we go?" Bill asked feigning enthusiasm.

"Right now my wife went to get the rental car and there she is now." Ted was pointing at a 1958 Chevy. The old car had seen better days.

"Okay let's go, I guess I can leave my luggage in the car." Bill introduced himself to the man's wife and entered the front seat next to the woman. The wife, Betty, looked at Bill in a weird way and then back at her husband who entered the back seat. Ted looked at his wife with a shrug of his shoulders.

"Honey Bill here is going to accompany us to the seminar."

"Oh that's nice Ted." The woman looked over at Bill who had a strange look on his face. Bill was eyeing the woman up and down as if she were a steak, or a nice car.

They drove for what seemed an eternity when they came out to a large field. There were several old cars and buses parked in the field. Bill looked at all the vehicles, taking note of the ones with the windows down. The best opportunity to take something was when they left the windows down and were distracted by a seminar. Bill, Ted and Betty made their way over to another field that joined the parking field. The temperature was high and the sun was beating down. Bill noticed his shirt was soaked with sweat. He made a mental note to grab another shirt out of a car that had a window down. He would feign interest in the seminar and then back peddle his way over to the parking lot. Then he would take advantage of the cars, and high tail it back to the hotel. Bill looked up at a stage that was set up across the field. There was a man on the stage ranting to a huge number of people in the field crowding the stage. He was going on about the end of days, and his people.

Bill turned to Ted, "I thought you said this was some kind of seminar, not a religious evangelist brainwashing."

Ted was staring at the stage, "Well I had heard this guy was real dynamic and spoke out on everything, not just religion. Let's give him a chance maybe he can make some sense out of this crazy world. I mean look at all those people listening to him. He can't be all bad if that many people are listening to him."

"Well you go on ahead I'm going to mosey around here. I noticed there were some tables back here with food on them." Bill claimed as he started his back peddling.

"Okay we'll catch you later." Ted yelled back to Bill as he and Betty moved up closer to the stage. Bill looked over his shoulder just in time to miss a young woman with a tray. She was holding the tray with one hand and pouring a drink into cups from a picture with the other.

"Would you like a beverage mister?" The woman asked.

"Sure would it's hot out here."

"Yeah, but I would go anywhere just to hear him speak, Mr. Jones is a great man." The girl said looking at the stage with dreamy eyes.

"Well, whatever just let me have some of that drink. What is it anyway?"

"Cool aid." The girl replied in a perky voice as Bill

sucked down his first of three cups.

FAME

The crowd cheers and people are moving around me. I slowly make my way to the stage waiting for my moment of fame. I listen to the yelling all around me, some people try to touch me while I am escorted down an aisle. I feel the excitement in the air, the nigh tangible energy that these people have brought with them to this event. Already there have been others on the stage and whence they came and went I shall aspire to fame. For it is I who have been chosen to use a new instrument, where as the others before me failed to inspire and incite this crowd with their archaic performance. I, who have been chosen to partake in this magnificent event, I who will know what it is like to be the center of attention for the first time in my life. The rest of my entourage is already in place waiting for my arrival to my position of honor. Everyone has prepared for this historic moment that shall go into the annuals for all time. I have reached the steps to the stage and slowly make my way. I feel the undulation of the crowd moving through my very being creating goose bumps on my skin. The crowd roars with a renewed surge of excitement as I reach the final step. I look around at all those present upon the stage and then I look to my instrument. There, in the middle of the platform, is my destiny. This shall be its maiden voyage. This shall be the first day of the mechanisms performance in front of a crowd. The people scream with their palpable excitement. Their words, which are yelled in French, are indiscernible to my ears. France, the birthplace of this magnificent invention; which shall entertain the masses. The French shall be honored by this day; when the people shall witness a new world being birthed before their eyes. The blood is pumping through my veins and I feel somewhat weak in the legs from the strain and pressure of this undertaking. Strong arms support me and encourage my forward progression. My fans await and I shall not disappoint them. The machine awaits its destiny, which shall ever be entwined with me. Our names shall be synonymous though all time. Then slowly as my congregation quiets down I enter into the contraption, poised to perform. As the tension builds to its pendulant climax the rope is pulled. I feel a rush of air and then dizzy, so dizzy. I look up

and there in front of me is my body encased in the guillotine.

Darkness ensconces my world, and my fame is sealed.

SHARKS

I coast out into the black and murky sea; surrounded by other
vessels that commune together toward a common destination.
We move in a pack, because this is the safest way to travel.
Each goads the other to move faster, the destination beckons us.
But what lurks in this sea, what searches for prey? The sharks
search for those to catch and pull under, for the unfortunates that
they deem palpable to their taste. They, the sharks, are driven
like a single machine to capture as many as they can. The only
reprieve for us fish is to move in our school and hope we are not
the unlucky ones. We pray every day that we are not the one to
get caught. We run the gambit, hoping the odds are in our favor.

I think to myself, "I won't get caught, but the poor guy
behind me or the one to my right and left, they will be the next
prey, not me. For days and days it goes on like this in an endless
cycle. We move in a school and then one of us gets caught, but
it has not been my day. I am the fish who gets away, I am that
lucky fish who beats the odds. Then suddenly it happens. My

day has come because there behind me is a shark. He has not caught me yet, but I see the look in his eyes. That hungry predator look that tells me, he is not going to let me go. I am his prey and he's toying with me before he strikes. My heart races and my pulse quickens. I think this is going to be it, I either go as fast as I can to escape the machine or give up and allow him to take me. The others will go on for another day, but today is my day and I realize that I can not hope to escape the speed and power of this shark. Maybe he won't continue to chase? Maybe, I think in the back of my mind, "Maybe he won't bite down, maybe he will go for the other prey on his right or behind?" Maybe is a vain reasoning, maybe is the reasoning before a bullet passes into a victims flesh or a car stalled on the train tracks just before the train hits it. Suddenly as my thoughts of maybe began the shark lurches forward to engulf me and I see the blue and red lights flash in the hypnotic dance that beckons the end of my progression with the pack. I pull my car to the side of the road and await the state trooper to write my ticket for speeding.

TOD

I despise Tod, such a horrible, cruel…..I will never forgive
Tod…never. Tod was at the emergency room when I
arrived there. It all started when I was at work earlier
today, I'm a cop working in NYC. I have been a cop for
over fifteen years and I've dealt with killers, rapists,
molesters…all sorts of monsters and evil, but never have I
hated something or someone as much as Tod. Today
started out like any other day where I kissed my wife and
kids, headed out to work with my partner, Roger. We work
homicide and today we received a call about a family
murder. We showed up at the scene a little after 0900
hours and to our surprise the bodies were still somewhat
warm. Rigor mortis was just starting to set in and the
adipose tissue wasn't built up on one side of the bodies.
The victims were a man and woman in their mid-fifties.
They were both executed with their hands tied behind their

backs, kneeling in their living room. We had a suspect in mind and that would be their son, who was missing from the house.

Roger told me he would search the bedrooms for clues and asked me to check out the lower level. I started walking a grid and made sure not to disturb anything that would screw up the CSI crew. I noticed a door off their kitchen in the back of the house and proceeded to open it. Stairs going down to a basement so I headed down them with my gun drawn. The locals cordoned off the house but didn't inspect it before we arrived so there was a chance the kid, who looked to be in his teens according to the pictures we looked at in the living room, could still be hiding in the house. I slowly proceeded down the stairs and immediately heard a disturbance behind some boxes near the rear of the basement. I gave him a chance by announcing that I was the police and the house was surrounded. If he gave himself up then he would be safe and I would give him whatever help he needed. He said he was scared and that he was afraid the man who killed his parents would come back so he hid in the basement. After some coaxing he came out from behind the boxes and apparently did not have a weapon on him. I questioned him about who the man he claimed killed his parents was and why he was spared. He claimed that the man was a business partner of his fathers and that they were doing something that probably wasn't quite legal but wasn't too sure. His father was very guarded about what he was doing and he over heard them talking about his father holding out on the man and that he promised to do something for the man and didn't do it. The boy claimed he heard the men arguing and he came down from his room to see what was going on. He noticed his parents were on their knees with their arms tied behind their backs while the man was pacing in front of them with a gun in his hand. He claimed the man was a cop or at least appeared to be one because he had a badge on his waist. Right at that moment I heard Roger

call down if I found anything and I shouted to him that I

found the kid. Roger proceeded down the stairs and the

boy's eyes went wide with fear. I knew at that moment that

I was in trouble, apparently Roger was running a scam on

the side and using this kids father to launder or resell seized

contraband…not sure if it was drugs or just laundering cash

but it was enough for Roger to put a gun, most likely a

plant gun that he will claim was the kids gun, and put two

slugs into my back. I went down like a rock…yeah I know

you were thinking Tod was who tried to end my life but no

Tod was later at the ER. Tod is on my shit list along with

Roger but that comes later. I went face first onto the

concrete floor and I could hear the kid crying and

screaming in the back ground…my ears were ringing from

the shots but I could still make out what was being said.

Basically it was along the lines of Roger telling the kid it

was unfortunate that he had seen him earlier and it wasn't

of any use to deny it since the kids look of fear was enough to tip me, his partner, off. He told the kid something shitty like sorry kid it's just business and proceeded to follow the kid as the teen started a slow backward retreat toward the furnace in the basement. As if the furnace would afford the kid some kind of protection…I guess it was just desperation but luck would have it that the kid actually made Roger move in front of me. All it took was me to raise my wrist with my gun in it and pull the trigger; which I did and that was how Roger lost the back of his head and the front all in the same instant. The kid was safe and I took some solace in that but I still was leaking my life fluid all over the basement floor. The officers outside heard the shots and came running in. I was lucid enough to let them know that the kid was innocent and Roger was doing some dirty shit. They took me to the closest emergency room and that is where I met Tod. I was rushed in and their were nurses and doctors all around me rushing to cut my clothes off and hook up an IV to me. The doctor made some demands about X-rays and running blood tests and getting plasma…etc…etc… It was very surreal, everything was somewhat blurry and people were all over me. I remembered looking over to my right between the doctors that were trying to stymie the flow of blood leaking out of me, and noticed a man on another gurney staring at me. I remember thinking that he was kind of rude just staring at me in a very vulnerable state. I thought he was an asshole who needed to mind his own business and that was when I first heard them mention Tod. So I figured that was the guy's name, the rude asshole that wouldn't stop staring at me. Until I notice that he didn't blink…ever….that man, Tod was not blinking…and looking kind of blue. The man was dead and here I was being pissed at him for being rude. I over heard a doctor yell at a nurse to get Mr. Reynold's body out of the ER. The nurse looked at the mans chart at the bottom of his gurney and said his name out loud to make sure she knew who she was taking. She said Steven Reynolds and then looked at the man with a sad look before placing a sheet over his head and wheeling him out of the ER. So his name wasn't Tod after all, I could remember thinking then who the hell is Tod…why did one of the doctors yell out Tod next to Steven Reynolds? Then I felt some pulling on my body and heard one of the doctors working on me scream, clear! I jumped up in the air and felt an incredible pain in my chest…shortly followed by him yelling, clear, again and then I jumped up in the air again. I could over hear a buzzing sound next to my ear. It was a steady blip sound earlier but now turned into a steady high pitched tone.

Things were starting to slip to blackness at that point and then I overheard the doctor yell out, "Tod! Come on people he's gone just give me the Tod….what the hell is the time of death?"

Son of a bitch do I hate Tod!

Interview with a Super Hero

"Well some things never change. Evil doers never seem to get the hint….it's funny you know…we beat their butts every time but they just feel the need to attempt another stupid plot to try and take over the world or destroy it and of course we always stop them. Okay, okay enough gloating let me get down to the brass tacks here. You are wanting to try out for our group but what do you have to offer?" Inquired Captain Powerful.

"Uhhh…I'm sorry what do you mean about having something to offer?" the confused man asked.

"You know, what do you have to offer? What special gift do you have? We don't just take anyone into our group. I mean, look, we have all kinds of fans groupies etc… even some of our nemesis that would love to infiltrate our legion of heroes. So I ask you again what do you have to offer and why should we let you into our fold?"

Captain Powerful asked while flexing his pectoral muscles. He knows that he must be an impressive visage with his rippling muscles and his long cape, though he tries not to be too imposing. He doesn't want to intimidate the poor man.

"Um…well I can..uh..can you give me an example? I mean what exactly can your legion do?" Questioned the man somewhat timidly.

"Hmmm…okay I will humor you but if this is some kind of trick that your masters have tasked you with in order to discover the flaws or weaknesses of us Super Heroes." Captain Powerful asked while placing his knuckles on the table and rising halfway out of his seat and flexing his muscles at the same time.

"No…no I'm just wondering what everyone else has for qualifications. So I can to see if I'm even in the same category as everyone else here." Hoping to have placated Captain Powerful's fearsome countenance.

" Okay fine, over by the window you have The Speedster. He can do anything in a vehicle with wheels. If he can make it go then no one can catch him…well no one normal anyway." Captain Powerful said while pointing at the man sitting in a chair at the window. The man in the chair by the window didn't even look at Captain Powerful even though the man was pointing at him and had a booming voice. Captain Powerful is very proud of his team.

"Over there next to the musical instruments is Ms….. Acrobati..ca..yeah Ms Acrobatica she…."

"Can do acrobats?" Said the hopeful candidate.

"Um..yeah but not just normal acrobats, she's the most acrobatic person in the world. She can flip up walls and jump from roof to roof and do flips off buildings." Captain Powerful beamed.

"Kind of like free runners." Said the small man

while shaking his head and feeling like he was catching on.

"What? What the hell are you talking about? What free runners?" Asked Captain Powerful while starting to get to his feet. Anger getting the better of him, feeling that the man was mocking him.

"I didn't mean anything by it. Free runners are people that can do what you described. They can jump from buildings and do flips off of high places." The man said explaining himself.

"Oh…um yeah like them but more so. She can do some incredible things with her body. Don't get any ideas though; she's got the hots for me." Said Captain Powerful impressed with himself. As though Don Juan had nothing on him.

"Uh sure."

"Okay so over there playing ping pong is The Mind. He can read people's thoughts and even make them do things. He can implant ideas and people will feel the need to do what he wants." He said while pointing at a bald man in a pink bathrobe. The man smiled and waved back at him with a smile on his face.

"Um...he kind of has the hots for me as well." Said the Captain, embarrassed.

"I see...well what other special individuals do you have on your team?" Inquired the small man to let Captain Powerful off the embarrassing situation.

"Yeah okay there's knives over there sitting by the television. He can stick any bulls eye with anything sharp. He never misses." Captain Powerful was pointing at a man sitting at a tray table who was in the process of putting butter on a muffin with a butter knife. The man glanced up and narrowed his eyes in a hateful manner at Captain Powerful.

"Uh...yeah he kind of has the hots for Ms. Acrobatica." The Captain confessed.

"Anyway so that is the team and now I ask you

once again. What can you do?" Captain Powerful pressed.

The man looked down at his hands and started to flex his fingers; which were interlaced while he was listening to Captain Powerful prattle on about his people.

"Well I have a confession to make. You see I now know about you and your team Captain Powerfool. And now I shall let it be known that not only do I scoff at your puny team of inept heros but I am here to infiltrate and destroy your group. You see I do work for the enemy, I work for the other side 4C ward. We are here to take your turf and to usurp your power. Hahahahahahahahahaha."

"Okay people that's the end of recreation time for 4B ward it's time for 4C ward to have it's time in the room. Let's go back to our rooms now." Yelled a man in scrubs. "The nurse will be administering your medications."

Captain Powerful looked at his new nemesis with shock in his eyes. "Deceiver, Judas, Benedict Arnold! I should have known it was a trick." cried Captain Powerful.

"You should have, you fool. Now it's time for my people to take over. 4C ward rules! Hahahah." The small man gloated in his victory.

"This isn't over!" Threatened Captain Powerful.

Gone Fishing

It is a clear and sunny day in southern Florida. I was at my usual fishing hole trying to catch the big one; which I do quite often…always on the look out for the one that got away. I like to get an early start so I say goodbye to the wife and kids and make my way to the spot that was passed down from my father and before him his father. Passed down from generation to generation and I'm hoping that soon it will be passed down to my children. So here I was trolling back and forth looking for the illusive fish that has gotten away from me for several years…we call it the whopper. My father also tried to catch this same fish and he always managed to elude him. We kind of feel like it knows when we are around and then avoids us. The whopper is playing us and has been for years…but some day I am going to catch him off guard and then I will mount his head on my wall…probably eat the rest. Hey, they are delicious fish in these parts.

So here I was on this beautiful sunny day enjoying my time fishing when I notice these guys troll up in their bass boat. For several generations this spot has been un-disturbed but for some reason today these two dorks decide to invade my fishing hole. I try to be big about it and ignore them but here they are in this forty thousand dollar boat and a cooler full of beer. They were loud as well…which meant they were scaring off all the fish. Any fisherman worth a damn knows you have to be quiet or you will scare off your prey. So not only were they pissing me off but here they were driving off all the quarry. I still thought I should behave and leave them to their stupidity; hell it's not like they were going to catch anything, morons. One started screaming and yelling then he threw the beer can up in the air and shot it with a pistol he was holding. So now I know that they are stupid and dangerous, someone could get hurt by these morons. I kept my distance and tried to be obscure, for the most part they left me alone to my fishing…although my fishing was pretty much shot due to these fools.

The day wore on and I hadn't caught a thing nor did the drunken fools since they were more preoccupied with their drinking and being stupid than fishing. This pissed me off even more since they obviously didn't depend on their fishing for food, but I do and so does my family.

I was getting ready to call it quits and head home since these dumb asses weren't going home anytime soon. Just as I was starting to leave I over hear one of them yell out that they had a bite. Then he said it was a big one. The other claimed it was the biggest fish he had ever seen. My blood ran cold, could they be referring to whopper? I approached them from the back so they didn't notice me and waited about ten feet from their boat. Then I saw it and my anger rose for there it was; the whopper and it was on their lines. The man was about to reel in my fish, the fish that my father and myself had tried to catch for several years and these two morons who came here for the first time, and drunk, had somehow caught my fish. The one that wasn't holding the fishing pole reached over the side of the boat to pull whopper in and that was when I made my decision. I wasn't going home empty handed. Yes, I know it's wrong to steal someone else's catch but enough was enough. I quickly moved toward them and grabbed the mans arm that was trying to pull whopper into the boat. I swallowed whopper whole and half of the man's arm.

I heard the other man scream, "Holy shit a shark!" I then circled the boat while the men were screaming and bumped it as hard as I could. Both men went into the water and I had finally caught something for the day.

www.ingramcontent.com/pod-product-compliance
Lightning Source LLC
Chambersburg PA
CBHW070931130626
46555CB00001B/388